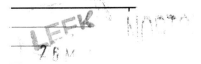

Staffordshire Library and Information Services
Please return or renew or by the la

LEEK

2 8 M

The Mystery of
Silver Falls

The whole town turns out to watch the first train journey when the bridge at Silver Falls is completed. The atmosphere is joyous, but the day turns sour when Kane Cresswell and his bandit gang arrive. They raid the train and, in the ensuing chaos, $50,000 falls into the river, seemingly lost forever.

Wyndham Shelford cannot get this image out of his head and is determined to find the missing money. Soon bodies start washing up in the river, and the unconventional lawman US Marshal Lloyd Drake arrives. The marshal believes that the train raid wasn't everything it seemed, but his reckless search for the truth is endangering the lives of everyone in town. Can Wyndham find the money and put a stop to this path of violence before it's too late?

By the same author

The Outlawed Deputy
The Last Rider from Hell
Death or Bounty
Bad Day in Dirtwood
Devine's Law
Yates's Dilemma
The Ten Per Cent Gang
Mendosa's Gun-Runners
Wanted: McBain
Six-shooter Bride
Dead by Sundown
Calhoun's Bounty
Calloway's Crossing
Bad Moon over Devil's Ridge
Massacre at Bluff Point
The Gallows Gang
Riders of the Barren Plains
Sharpshooter McClure
Railroad to Redemption
Bleached Bones in the Dust
The Secret of Devil's Canyon
The Prairie Man
Sheriff Without a Star
The Search for the Lone Star
Beyond Redemption
Devine
Night of the Gunslinger
The Devil's Marshal
Legend of the Dead Men's Gold
Bullet Catch Showdown
All Must Die

The Mystery of Silver Falls

I.J. Parnham

A Black Horse Western

ROBERT HALE · LONDON

ISBN 978-0-7198-1626-0

Robert Hale Limited
Clerkenwell House
Clerkenwell Green
London EC1R 0HT

www.halebooks.com

Typeset by
Derek Doyle & Associates, Shaw Heath
Printed and bound in Great Britain by
CPI Antony Rowe, Chippenham and Eastbourne

CHAPTER 1

'It's my great pleasure to declare the final stretch of rail track open,' Finnegan Kelly announced. 'And I'm confident the new bridge will herald an era of prosperity for Silver Falls.'

Finnegan carried on speaking, but the cheering crowd drowned out his words. Then the engine delivered a lengthy blast on the whistle before the train lurched into motion, forcing everyone to rush away from the tracks.

Standing on the edge of the platform, Wyndham Shelford had mixed feelings about today's ceremony, and the sour expression on the face of his colleague Crosby Jensen suggested he, too, was having misgivings. While the bridge at Silver Falls was being built, Wyndham and Crosby, along with five other men, had provided security for the site.

The work had been uneventful as, aside from a few thefts, there had been no trouble. Now that the job was complete, they were out of work and so Wyndham would welcome a few more months of routine, paid employment.

Despite his concern, he joined the townsfolk of Silver Falls in cheering the train as it trundled out of the station to embark on its five-mile journey to the bridge and then beyond for the very first time.

When the last car moved away from the platform, most of the crowd hurried after it while waving their hats above their heads. Then several riders appeared from town and they flanked the train while shooting into the air.

Within moments the crowd thinned out, leaving Wyndham and Crosby standing at one end of the platform and Finnegan standing at the other.

'Where's the free liquor?' someone asked from behind Wyndham. He turned to find that his friend Gareth Wilson had joined them along with most of their colleagues who had provided security for the bridge.

'I thought you were staying at the bridge to watch the first train go across,' Wyndham said.

'We were,' Gareth said, 'but then Finnegan Kelly sent us a message that the drinks in the Station Saloon would be free for the rest of the day.'

'They are.' Wyndham looked around. 'Where's Ewan Douglas?'

'He decided to board the train and be one of the first across.' Gareth looked past Wyndham and picked out Finnegan. 'Come on. The quicker we get our old boss to the saloon, the quicker we can start drinking.'

Everyone laughed as they joined Gareth in hurrying across the platform. Wyndham joined them, but as he wasn't as eager to get some liquor in him as the others were, he looked again at the train.

The people on foot had now slowed to a halt, but the riders were still flanking the train, looking as if they would accompany it all the way to the bridge.

It may have been Wyndham's recent work that made him uneasy, as for the last few months he had been suspicious of everything, but he didn't think anyone should be so excited that they would ride along beside the train.

So he watched the riders until a rise took them and the train out of sight. Then, with a shake of the head, he dismissed the matter and hurried on to join his friends.

The moment the train brakes screamed Ewan Douglas made his move.

The two bandits guarding the door lurched forward, but Ewan let the sudden deceleration propel him from his chair. He stood tall and before either bandit could right himself, he drew his Peacemaker.

Two crisp gunshots rang out. The first caught the left-hand bandit in his gun arm while the second sliced into the other bandit's chest, dropping him.

As Ewan moved down the aisle towards them, the wounded man struggled to raise his gun and so Ewan dispatched him with a deadly shot to the head. Then he turned to face the passengers.

'I'm a bridge security guard,' he said. 'So you folks have nothing to fear now. Just stay here and I'll deal with the others.'

He caught the eyes of several people and when they provided relieved smiles he moved on to the door. He hoped that the squealing brakes had masked the gunfire, leaving the rest of the bandits feeling confident, but the fact that they were making the train perform an unscheduled stop suggested he had to act quickly.

He glanced through the inset window. Nobody was outside and so he slipped through and then made his way to the door to the last car.

A blind had been drawn down over the window, but the inside of the car was well lit, letting him see the outlines of men moving around. This suggested that the bandits had already opened the other door in readiness for a fast departure.

Ewan looked down the length of the train. The engine was about to trundle on to the bridge across the Black River. He judged that when the train stopped the bulk of the train would be on the bridge while the end car would be ten yards from land.

This left him with about three minutes to make his move. He used the first minute to check on either side of the train.

He couldn't see anyone waiting for them, but this raid had been well organized, even if he didn't know what the bandits were planning to steal. As he waited to make his move, he couldn't help but smile at the irony of this situation.

During the construction of the bridge he had encountered few problems. Then, on the inaugural train journey, and a few hours after he'd been paid off, the train had just left the town of Silver Falls when, in a co-ordinated move, bandits had made their presence known.

Several riders who had been flanking the train in apparent celebration had moved in and boarded the end car. At the same time, the bandits who had mingled in with passengers had seized control of the train without trouble.

In truth, dealing with this problem was no longer his responsibility and he didn't have the help of his trusted friends, but he dismissed that concern with a shrug.

The end car was twenty yards from the bridge when Ewan reached for the door. By then he could see down to the rapidly flowing river below that ended abruptly several hundred yards on at the waterfall that had given the town of Silver Falls its name.

He tore his gaze away from the scenery and burst in through the door. The scene was just as he'd imagined it.

The four railroad guards were bound and sitting on the floor on either side of the car, while two men were dragging a strongbox out through the door. They glanced up while smiling, clearly anticipating seeing their fellow bandits.

Their smiles died when Ewan jerked up his gun, and with both men having their hands on the strongbox, he hammered a shot into the chest of one of the men before either could retaliate. As the wounded man slumped over the strongbox, Ewan swung the gun to the side, but the second man stepped out of view on to the platform at the back of the car.

The strongbox had been in a precarious position on the edge of the platform, but then the brakes squealed insistently, making the train lurch. The wounded man slipped away and a moment later the strongbox followed him in, toppling from immediate view.

Ewan reckoned that when the train stopped the men who had taken control of the engine would arrive, but he still moved on cautiously while reloading. Then he saw a shadow move beyond the door that he took for the other man jumping off the train, and so he speeded up.

When he next caught sight of the man, he couldn't help but smile. The strongbox had taken an unfortunate deflection off the rail tracks and that had moved it towards the side of the bridge.

The strongbox was still tumbling end over end,

and Ewan judged that it was moving quickly enough for it to topple over the edge. But its momentum died out at the point where it was standing on its end and one more movement would make it drop from sight altogether.

The bandit reached the strongbox and went to his knees while slapping a hand on the side, securing it. Then he swung round to look at the train, and it was to find Ewan standing in the doorway with his gun already trained on him.

Ewan gave a warning shake of the head and so the bandit raised his free hand. The train was still moving when Ewan jumped down.

'This sure is an unfortunate turn of events,' he said as he walked down the tracks. 'Who are you? And what's in the strongbox?'

'I'm Kane Cresswell,' the man said. 'And there's fifty thousand dollars in silver in the box. It's the railroad's last payment now the work's done, except now it's mine.'

Ten yards from the strongbox, Ewan stopped beside the man he had shot. He noted that the man was lying still and then looked up.

'I've never heard of you. Yours wasn't one of the names the railroad mentioned, and they said the other potential troublemakers were devious varmints. Clearly you're not.'

Ewan laughed, making Kane snarl at him.

'I planned this raid down to the last detail and I'll

still walk away with the silver.' Kane nodded down the bridge. 'The moment the train stops, the rest of my men will come down off the engine and they'll cut you to ribbons.'

'You don't give the orders here. Get on your feet and step away from the strongbox!'

As behind him Ewan heard the train shudder to a halt, he and Kane locked gazes. Kane was the first to glance away and with a resigned shrug he raised his other hand.

Kane glared defiantly at Ewan as he got up on one knee. Then he moved to stand up, but instead of rising he jerked down behind the strongbox. Ewan was alert to Kane's likely response and he blasted a shot at him.

Kane moved too quickly and the shot thudded into the metal rim of the strongbox, sending up sparks. Hunkered down, only the top of Kane's hat was visible as Ewan walked to the side.

He was confident of what Kane's next move would be, and sure enough Kane slapped his gun hand on the strongbox and fired wildly around the area where Ewan had been standing. He got in two shots before Ewan fired.

Ewan aimed at Kane's fingers, but the bullet nicked the barrel of the gun, jerking it out of Kane's hand. Kane stumbled into view while wringing his hand, but only for a moment as he nudged against the strongbox and toppled it over.

12

The strongbox rocked down towards the edge of the bridge and despite Ewan's previous comments he didn't want to lose the money. He hurried forward aiming to save the strongbox, but thankfully Kane was quick-witted and lithe enough to still its progress.

He grabbed a post with one hand and then, with a mixture of his other arm and his legs, he brought the strongbox to a halt. Even so, when the strongbox stopped moving it was angled over the edge of the bridge with only Kane keeping it from falling.

Ewan moved round to stand behind Kane where he could look down on him while looking along the bridge. As Kane had promised, the other bandits had come out of the engine and they were moving forward.

'Help me get this back up,' Kane said, glancing over his shoulder.

Ewan noted the sweat on Kane's brow and his strained muscles.

'You're doing fine on your own. Just keep pushing and you'll—'

Ewan broke off when a ferocious burst of gunfire came from further down the bridge, the possibility of the imminent loss of the strongbox forcing the bandits to act. As lead sliced into the brickwork before him, Ewan hunkered down and took aim at the nearest bandit, but just then hot fire punched him in the chest.

The next he knew he was looking up at the sky and

13

what felt like a heavy weight was pressing down on his chest. With a supreme effort he rolled on to his side to lie on the edge of the bridge where he was confronted by Kane's grinning face.

'They got you,' he said with relish. 'And your last sight will be us riding off with the silver.'

Ewan couldn't drag enough air into his lungs to reply and he could only watch as Kane shifted position to raise the box. Then, with a sudden lurch, the strongbox slipped down.

Kane arrested its movement and for a frozen moment he and the strongbox stayed still. Then his hand lost its grip of the post and he and the strongbox fell.

While only moving his head, Ewan followed their progress and watched as both man and money tumbled towards the moiling waters below.

They hit the surface of the water, sending up two surprisingly small splashes. A few heartbeats later the disturbances on the water dissipated, lost amidst the waves.

Ewan could hear the other bandits hurrying down the bridge, but the sounds appeared to be coming from a great distance. He figured he was in big trouble, but he'd always enjoyed looking at the river and so he fixed his gaze on the water.

A minute passed before he caught sight of Kane's body. He was already several hundred yards away and he appeared to be lying face down in the water trapped in an eddy behind a floating tree trunk.

Then the trunk plummeted over the falls and a few moments later Kane followed it. With nothing left to see, Ewan closed his eyes.

CHAPTER 2

'The train got raided,' Norman Pierce announced.

He continued to explain, but Wyndham Shelford struggled to hear him. Like Finnegan Kelly earlier, the crowd drowned out his speech, although unlike before everyone was concerned rather than excited.

Ten minutes ago a rumour that something had gone wrong at the bridge had reached the Station Saloon and Finnegan, along with several other railroad men, had hurried away. Every few minutes a new rumour had arrived, ranging from the train breaking down on the bridge to the bridge collapsing.

Now the boss of the railroad office appeared to have definitive news and so the bartender, Benny Stokes, encouraged everyone to quieten by insistently banging a glass on the bar. When silence had descended and all eyes had turned to Norman, he got up on the bar.

'Bandits raided the train on the bridge,' he said.

16

'There was plenty of shooting and several bandits were killed. Finnegan Kelly will be back soon with the full story.'

The customers cheered, although Norman's pensive expression suggested that it wasn't all good news. As he got down off the bar, everyone returned to exchanging animated conversation, but when Gareth Wilson noticed that Wyndham wasn't joining in, he looked at him oddly.

'I reckon I might have seen the bandits,' Wyndham said with a frown. 'These men rode out of town and they left flanking the train.'

'I didn't see them,' Gareth said.

Crosby nudged him in the ribs. 'That's because you were too busy looking for the free drinks.'

Most of the others had seen the riders, although that didn't clarify whether these men were the bandits. A lull in the chatter in the saloon curtailed their discussion and when Wyndham turned around, Finnegan Kelly had arrived.

Even before he reached the bar Finnegan's thunderous expression and the tense postures of the railroad men with him showed that the full story he had to tell would be a troubling one.

'The bandits were led by Kane Cresswell,' Finnegan announced in the quiet saloon, making several people shrug and murmur that the name meant nothing. 'Kane was killed along with several other bandits. The survivors fled.'

Finnegan frowned and with him not saying anything more, Benny Stokes took it upon himself to
make the obvious comment.

'We can tell you have bad news,' he said. 'You'd
better let us have it.'

Finnegan cast his measured gaze around the
room.

'Kane was after the fifty thousand dollars in silver
that was on the train.' Finnegan raised his voice
when the customers gasped in surprise. 'The money
was the railroad's final payment to its backers after
the completion of the bridge. In the confusion the
money fell off the train and then fell off the bridge.
It's no doubt been lost for ever.'

'Why keep that payment a secret?' Norman asked.
'And why take it on the train's maiden journey?'

Finnegan swirled round to glare at Norman and
he pointed a stern finger at him.

'You no longer work for the railroad.' Finnegan
then glared at people individually, picking out railroad workers and daring them to retort. When
nobody met his eye, he snorted in irritation. 'Then
I'll turn this around. Anyone who still wants to work
for me had better come up with a useful idea.'

Wisely, nobody drew attention to themselves,
although when Finnegan moved his angry gaze
round to Wyndham's group, Gareth spoke up, his
tone lilting after all the free liquor he'd consumed.

'Were the bandits those men who rode out of

town?' he asked. 'Because there were these riders and we wondered if they might have been Kane Cresswell and his. . . .'

Gareth trailed off when Finnegan glowered at him, confirming that trying to be helpful in this situation wasn't sensible.

'I can confirm those riders were the bandits, but you're one of the men I paid to look after security and you did nothing when you saw a bandit gang ride to raid the train.'

Gareth shrugged. 'You paid us off this morning.'

Wyndham laughed as did several others, but Gareth's inappropriate attempt to make light of the situation made Finnegan gesture at his ever-present hired gun, Marvin Reynolds. Marvin made his way through the crowded saloon with his shoulders hunched.

Wyndham's group bunched up to meet the threat, but Marvin didn't even reach them. Several customers closed ranks to rebuff him and when Marvin tried to advance, they knocked him away.

Marvin shoved back and aimed a wild punch at the nearest man. A messy fight of the kind that had often broken out in here would have then erupted, but with the customers being packed together tightly, those involved in the altercation could only edge back and forth.

With nobody making progress Finnegan called for calm. After a few more shoves and a couple of punches, Marvin returned to join Finnegan, whose face was now bright red with suppressed anger.

'Does anyone know anything about these riders?' he shouted.

Long moments passed without anyone offering a response. So, seeking to make amends after Gareth's badly received joke, Wyndham raised a hand.

'I don't reckon they were from town,' he said. 'They appeared out of nowhere and rode off at speed. I reckon Kane figured that the best way to allay suspicions during the celebration was to make sure he was seen.'

Half of the saloon murmured in agreement and the other half shrugged, suggesting they hadn't seen the men.

Finnegan sneered. 'I don't agree. I reckon Kane's plan was to fool the men I paid to maintain security.'

'He fooled everyone, including you.'

This time the whole saloon murmured in support, making Finnegan snarl.

'This town is filled with fools, but no longer.'

Finnegan whispered instructions to Marvin and he hurried away to clear a path to the door. Finnegan's other men surrounded him as he moved off through the saloon.

With Finnegan looking as if he'd depart on a sour note, Benny Stokes shouted after him.

'What are you planning to do?' he called.

Finnegan kept walking until he reached the

doorway where he swirled round. His measured response suggested he'd intended to have the final word before Benny had spoken.

'I'm holding you all responsible for that raid,' he said levelly. 'With the bridge work finished, the station would have ensured Silver Falls' prosperity, but no longer. This station will now close and trains will no longer stop here.'

With that, he turned on his heel and beat a hasty retreat. For several moments silence reigned and then angry questions flew back and forth as everyone tried to work out if they'd heard Finnegan correctly and if they had, whether he would carry out his threat.

Nobody provided a definitive answer and so several men hurried outside after Finnegan. This movement started a stampede of people heading for the door, but Wyndham's group stayed back.

'Those first men through the door looked angry enough to lynch him,' Wyndham said.

'They did,' Crosby said, 'but I'm more worried about them being angry enough to lynch us.'

Wyndham winced. 'I don't reckon what we said made Finnegan come to that decision. He'd have already decided to make scapegoats out of the towns-folk.'

He looked around for support. When he received shrugs and sighs, they headed to the window.

The scene outside was as Wyndham had expected

it with Finnegan and his men hurrying for their horses, pursued by most of the town.

Whether or not they caught up with him, Wyndham reckoned the response had ensured Finnegan would make good his threat. The railroad didn't need a station here and without it, the town would struggle.

Finnegan had reached his horse when Norman Pierce joined them. Norman had rarely spoken to them before and so he stood nervously rocking from foot to foot until they turned to him.

'Finnegan didn't tell you the full story,' he said. 'He dealt only with the bad news for the railroad.'

Wyndham considered Norman's downcast eyes and when the others picked up on his mood, they stood tall and faced him soberly.

'Ewan was on the train,' Wyndham said. 'Is it about him?'

'I'm afraid so. It seems Ewan got it into his head to take on the bandits single-handed. He killed several of them, but the rest overcame him. I'm sorry to bring you the bad news.'

'You don't need to be sorry when Finnegan didn't have the guts to tell us to our faces.'

Norman nodded and then made his way back to the bar.

'That sounds like Ewan,' Wyndham said after a while. 'Taking on a whole heap of bandits and not caring about the danger.'

'He was a good man,' Crosby said, making everyone murmur in agreement.

'So now there's only six of us,' Gareth said.

This thought made everyone sigh, but Wyndham shook his head.

'I reckon I'll stay here for a while,' he said. 'After what happened to Ewan, I need to do something different.'

'We all agreed to stay together after completing the job,' Gareth said. 'And it'll be quiet here without the bridge workers and with no station. In three months this place could be a ghost town.'

'It could, but I've been paid, so I don't have to hurry to find work. I'll rest up and read a few books, and I might look for the silver. While I've been here I've watched the river every day and I know the terrain. That silver has to pop up somewhere and I'd back my judgement to be there when it does.'

'Then I wish you luck.' Gareth leaned towards him. 'But if you find it, don't tell Finnegan in the hope he'll give you a reward.'

'I sure won't. The only people I'll share my good fortune with is my friends, so make sure you head back this way again one day.'

'We'll do that and if you don't find the silver, you can always join up with us again one day.'

Wyndham nodded and with that thought cheering him, he returned to watching Finnegan's hasty departure while the townsfolk grouped up to shout abuse and hurl anything that came to hand at him.

'Either way,' he said, 'I never want to see that man again.'

'So why do you think Finnegan was so annoyed with the townsfolk?' Crosby Jensen asked when everyone aside from Wyndham had congregated in the shack that overlooked the bridge.

Gareth Wilson shrugged, as did the others before they returned to sharing thoughts about their friend Ewan's demise.

For the last year, while they'd looked after security, this had been their base. The shack was set to the side of the bridge and it commanded a good view of the bridge, river and surrounding terrain.

Crosby reckoned the excellence of this vantage point was the main reason why they'd seen no trouble and now that the work was over he'd miss the nights they'd sat here. They had chatted, gambled and drank, so the work had hardly felt like work at all.

'Bandits raided the train and he had to blame someone,' Gareth said. 'Beyond that, we're moving on, so we shouldn't worry about it.'

'Wyndham's staying.'

'He is.' Gareth sighed. 'So now there's only five.'

Crosby frowned, deciding at that moment not to waste another moment before making his own announcement. He faced the group.

'Actually,' he said, 'that should be "now there's only four".'

Gareth winced. 'You're not staying with us either?'

'Like Wyndham, I've had a hankering to do something different and Ewan's death feels like the right moment to do it. A bounty is sure to get posted on the heads of this bandit gang, and maybe I should be the one to collect it.'

Crosby had expected his idea would generate ridicule, but instead his friends nodded knowingly, as if they'd somehow known he'd do this before he had decided himself.

'Which means Wyndham will search for the silver, while you'll search for the men who shot up Ewan. I hope you both find what you're looking for, and when you find them, make them regret what they did.'

Everyone murmured in support of this opinion, making Crosby sigh with relief.

'I will. So do you have any ideas where I can start looking?'

'Why would we have any ideas?' Gareth said with a frown.

'Because lots of things about that raid are odd. For a start Finnegan overreacted.' Crosby waved an arm as he warmed to his theme. 'And he paid us off early, which meant we weren't sitting here as we would have been doing when the raid happened.'

'I wish we had been. Then we could have helped

Ewan take on Kane Cresswell, but we didn't leave because Finnegan paid us off. It was because we'd heard about the free liquor in town.'

'Which is also suspicious. Finnegan's not a generous man.'

Gareth laughed. 'I can see you'll do well in your new life, but save the questioning until you get those bandits in your sights.'

With everyone murmuring that they agreed, Crosby dismissed his misgivings with a sigh. As he didn't want to make his leaving a protracted process, he shook everyone's hands and moved on to his horse.

Once he was mounted up, he looked back and smiled on seeing everyone now sitting in the doorway looking at the bridge, as they'd always done. Then he rode off.

He had no idea yet about how he would search for the bandits. But he figured he should first try Wyndham's idea of using his knowledge of the vagaries of Black River to see if he could find either the silver or Kane Cresswell's body.

The bank on this side was more treacherous than the other side and so he couldn't get close to the water until he'd moved past the falls. There he stopped and looked upriver, running his gaze along the quieter stretches of water where debris often washed up.

He saw nothing of interest, but that didn't stop

him riding downriver for several more miles. After his third stop without seeing anything untoward he headed back upriver, figuring that he'd seen enough and that this process had let him say his goodbyes to the river.

He resolved to veer away before he reached the bridge so that he wouldn't have to pass the shack, but when he approached the elevated land before the tracks smoke was spiralling up into the sky. He hurried up and when he crested the high point he identified the source of the fire as being the shack.

Concerned now, he hurried down the slope, across the tracks, and on to the shack. By the time he arrived, the building was an inferno, but he could see through the door and nobody was trapped inside.

He assumed his friends had decided that destroying the shack was a suitable way to end their time here and so he looked around, but he couldn't see them. He moved on, but he still looked over his shoulder until the tendrils of smoke receded into the distance.

CHAPTER 3

Three months later. . . .

'I'm looking for someone,' the newcomer said when the bartender Benny Stokes had filled his whiskey glass.

'Who's looking for this "someone"?' Benny asked.

'I'm Seymour Banks.'

Benny considered him and then pointed.

'Wyndham Shelford is sitting at the other end of the bar.'

Seymour looked where the bartender had indicated and found that Wyndham had glanced up from the Jules Verne novel he was reading to consider him. He tipped his hat, making Seymour turn back to Benny.

'How did you know who I was looking for?'

Benny gave Seymour a long look and then returned to polishing an already clean glass. Seymour downed his whiskey and moved along the bar to join Wyndham.

Wyndham marked his page by folding down a corner and then put down his book. He stood up while drinking the glass of water he'd been nursing.

'I charge a dollar a day, in advance,' he said, 'no matter how much of the day I spend showing you around.'

'How do you know what I. . . ?' Seymour trailed off. He fished a dollar out of his pocket and then directed Wyndham to lead the way.

When they were outside and walking down the main drag, Wyndham leaned towards Seymour.

'The only reason anyone comes to Silver Falls these days is to see where the silver fell.' Wyndham laughed. 'They're all surprised that anyone else might have had the same idea.'

Seymour offered a laugh of his own, although Wyndham could tell his reaction had disappointed him in the same way it always disappointed the others who came here in search of the fortune.

'I guess this makes me look foolish?'

'Nope, just hopeful. It's yet to be proven if you're lucky, too.'

With this thought making Seymour smile, they walked through town.

'This is a nice place, but is it always this quiet?' Seymour asked, clearly noting that they were the only people outside.

'It has been for the last three months.' Wyndham

29

sighed. 'After the raid the town paid a heavy price. As the raid started from here the railroad blamed us. Finnegan Kelly closed down the Silver Falls station.'

'So the town was called Silver Falls before the raid?'

'With the benefit of hindsight it was unfortunately named, but, as you'll see, the name's appropriate. The water coming over the falls looks silvery. Either way, three months on from the station being closed, only a handful of us is left eking out an existence in a town built for ten times our numbers.'

'That's terrible.' Seymour thought for a moment. 'But I'm not paying you any more.'

Wyndham chuckled. 'That's fine, but before you leave have another drink and something to eat in the Station Saloon.'

'I'll do that, unless I get lucky and decide to stay.'

Wyndham nodded and then with them about to embark on the journey down into Silver Gorge to the base of the falls he launched into his standard explanation.

As they walked along, he described the area as well as relating the tale about the raid and its conclusion that most people knew, with the added benefit of being able to point out the bridge and Black River.

By the time the higher section of the river disappeared from view as they moved down Silver Gorge, Seymour was already frowning as he accepted the harsh terrain made finding the silver a virtual impossibility.

'And so,' Wyndham said when they reached the bottom of the falls, 'what happened to the silver after that remains a mystery.'

Seymour moved forward while peering up at the curved wall of water that cascaded down into a seemingly boiling pool below. Although when he reached the edge, he couldn't help but notice the water was calmer closer to the shore.

'What's your best guess?' Seymour glanced over his shoulder and raised a hand when Wyndham started to reply. 'And I know everyone must ask you that.'

'They do, and I tell them the truth that I don't know.' Wyndham slipped a hand in his pocket and joined Seymour on the side of the water. 'And of course if I knew where the silver ended up, I wouldn't earn a living by charging folk a dollar a day to help them look for it.'

'But still, for a dollar a day, you can help me to avoid wasting my time, or at least stop me getting myself killed.'

Wyndham placed his free hand on Seymour's shoulder and gestured, indicating the falls, then the pool, and then the river beyond.

'The last anyone saw of the strongbox of silver dollars was it dropping into the river. It was heavy and would have sunk, but eventually the current would have sent it along the river bottom and over the edge. If the strongbox survived the drop – and I

31

reckon it should have – it'd have either carried on downriver towards Black Town, or it might have lodged somewhere closer to hand.'

Wyndham finished his explanation, pointing at a calm patch on the surface a hundred feet out into the water while he waited for the question they all asked these days.

'What about the silver dollars that have washed up recently?'

Wyndham leaned towards him and, while removing his hand from his pocket, he lowered his voice to a conspiratorial tone.

'They were found on this very spot.'

Wyndham looked around the water's edge, as if he might see one of those offerings, but Seymour didn't look down as he considered the calm water.

'Which would suggest the strongbox broke up, and so trying to find the whole hoard is a waste of time.'

'Sadly that is the case, although it's possible that only a handful escaped and they washed ashore.'

'I'd prefer that answer.' Seymour rubbed his jaw. 'It's certainly more appealing than the possibility that you planted the coins down here and then found them to make it appear that the strongbox is still close by.'

Seymour turned to him and Wyndham met his gaze for as long as he could without blinking. Then he turned to look at the water, while using the movement to disguise his placing a foot over the silver dollar he'd just dropped on the ground.

'It certainly is,' he said levelly.

Seymour dismissed the matter with a shrug and returned to looking at the water.

'What happens to similar objects that go over the falls?'

Wyndham slapped his back and then pointed at the calm patch.

'Now that's a good question. Last year, when I was working for the railroad, a wagon fell off the bridge. The river swallowed it up along with the wagon driver. Three months later I was down here when up pops the wagon. Then a few moments later, up pops the body.'

Seymour winced with a look of horror that made Wyndham think he was improving as a storyteller. Then Seymour pointed at the water, indicated a hunched form that was slowly turning round in the current.

'Would that be like the body that's just popped up over there?' he asked.

Herman Trask had made camp an hour ago, but he hadn't settled down yet.

Crosby had watched him from the scrub, waiting for the moment when he was vulnerable, but Herman was twitchy. Every few minutes he jerked around to look in all directions even though Crosby was still and silent in the dark.

Then again, over the last three months the remaining members of the Kane Cresswell gang hadn't fared well.

Crosby had learnt that originally there had been eight men in the bandit gang. Ewan Douglas had shot up three men during the failed train raid.

After the leader, along with the silver, had plunged over Silver Falls, the four surviving gang members had fled. US Marshal Lloyd Drake had been tasked with bringing them in, so they'd split up, but that hadn't helped them.

One man had doubled back to Black River where he'd done what Crosby had done and taken in the lie of the land, presumably hoping the strongbox had washed ashore.

By the time he'd turned away, accepting the roaring water made searching too dangerous, a bounty hunter had sneaked up on him. That man had joined Kane in plunging into the water, except this time he had several bullets in him.

The second man had the same idea, although he was more cautious. It didn't help him.

He sidled into Black Town, the nearest settlement downriver to Silver Falls, and sought out local knowledge about Black River. He had hoped to work out what fate might have befallen the money, but he asked too many questions.

The townsfolk became suspicious and joined

forces to gun him down. After that, the surviving two men abandoned trying to find the lost money quickly and fled.

The first man had the misfortune to hole up in Harmony where Crosby happened to be in the saloon. He had the further misfortune to come into the saloon while Crosby was examining his likeness on a Wanted poster.

Crosby's first, and what would probably be his easiest, bounty encouraged Crosby to search for his second bounty in the form of Herman Trask, the last gang member, but the chase had been a long one. The nervous Herman had kept moving and he'd been careful, but he had never strayed far from Silver Falls and that had been his downfall.

This encounter was the first time Crosby had got him in his sights.

Darkness had fallen when Crosby moved even closer, so the only light came from the small campfire. Herman was showing no sign of relaxing and so Crosby took his time in crawling towards him.

He was ten yards away with only thin scrub separating them when Herman flinched and leapt to his feet. He drew his gun and spun round, seemingly aware that someone was close, but not knowing where he was hiding.

Then he abandoned trying to work it out and splayed wild gunfire into the scrub. Thankfully, the slugs sliced into the ground several yards to Crosby's right, but Herman was sure to get lucky soon and so Crosby drew his gun.

Herman must have seen the movement as he fired off a shot that whistled over Crosby's right shoulder. Then he hightailed it away in the opposite direction, even vaulting the fire in his haste to get away.

Crosby loosed off a shot at his fleeing form, but the firelight dazzled him and the shot was wild. When Herman kept running, Crosby slapped the ground in irritation and leapt to his feet to give chase.

Herman was twenty yards away and he was on the edge of the circle of firelight, but after a few more paces the darkness swallowed him up. Despite the feeling that this hunt could go badly wrong, Crosby's heart was thudding with the thrill of the chase and he gave no thought to being cautious as he followed Herman into the darkness.

He caught fleeting glimpses of Herman's form and he heard him scrambling through the undergrowth. Herman was following an erratic path, veering to either side with no apparent clear direction.

Crosby followed and he reckoned he was gaining on him when, in a shocking moment, he registered that he could no longer hear Herman's frantic progress. He dug in a heel and came to a skidding halt a moment before Herman loomed up close, facing him with the glint of gunmetal in his hand.

Gunfire blasted from only four feet away, a shot that would have torn him in two if he'd kept running. Crosby reacted quickly and fired low, catching Herman in the stomach.

Herman doubled over while wasting a second shot into the ground. Then Crosby's second shot to the chest downed him.

In the inky darkness Herman disappeared from view and so Crosby moved rapidly to the side and then stood still as he waited to confirm that he'd dispatched his target.

'Who are you?' Herman asked after a while, his voice weak and pained.

Crosby edged closer until he saw Herman's form. He judged that he was lying on his back, but he didn't reply until a stray beam of light picked out Herman's gun lying on the ground.

'I'm Crosby Jensen,' he said. 'The Kane Cresswell gang shot up my friend Ewan Douglas and so I decided to mop up the last of the gang.'

Herman didn't respond immediately, but Crosby reckoned he was trying to make him overconfident so he would come closer, so he waited. Then Herman chuckled and that grew into laughter, albeit interspersed with wheezing and gasping.

'You've got to let a dying man enjoy himself,' Herman said when the laughter died out.

'What's so funny about dying?'

'Because you think I'm the last one.' Herman

snorted a laugh and took a deep breath. 'I'm not. Others are still out there and they'll come for you.'

Herman sounded so confident that Crosby swirled round, fearing that he'd walked into a trap, and Herman must have heard him move as he laughed again.

Crosby backed away while looking around into the darkness and it took him several minutes before he accepted that Herman's taunt wouldn't give him immediate problems.

Crosby returned to Herman's body, but when he reached him he was now still. Crosby shrugged and lugged the body on to a shoulder.

On his way back to the camp, like Herman earlier, he started at every night noise. Even when he dumped the body beside the fire, his heart continued to thud with an insistent rhythm.

CHAPTER 4

'Who is he?' Benny Stokes asked, eyeing the wrapped-up body with distaste.

'I have no idea,' Wyndham said. 'I avoided looking at him too closely, but I could tell he'd been in the water for some time.'

Benny grunted that he agreed while the others glanced at each other, each person clearly hoping someone else would take control of the situation.

After finding the body, Wyndham had returned to town and collected a blanket and rope. He had gone back down into the gorge on his own but, as had happened last year with the unfortunate man who had fallen off the bridge, the body had drifted to the water's edge on its own.

Seymour Banks had been standing vigil over it and they'd done their best to wrap the body up in the blanket in a dignified manner and take it out of Silver Gorge. Now it was lying in a corner of the saloon.

The time and effort involved in moving the body had ensured that the ten people who comprised Silver Falls' total population had gathered for this grim discussion. With nobody offering an opinion, Norman Pierce moved forward and knelt beside the body.

Norman was the nearest the town had to an authority figure. He had once run the railroad office in town, but he was the first man Finnegan Kelly had sacked and so he'd stayed here.

With a deep breath Norman unwrapped the blanket and considered the body before placing the blanket back over him.

'There's not enough left to recognize him,' he said.

The people who had glanced at the body, albeit from a greater distance, offered supportive murmurs.

'So unless someone comes here to ask about a missing person,' Wyndham said, 'we'll probably never know who he is.'

Norman raised a hand. 'Don't jump to conclusions. We might still be able to work this out. Has anyone ever gone missing before?'

Several people shrugged before looking at Wyndham, who appeared to have been appointed spokesman after finding the body.

'People left here in a hurry after Finnegan Kelly made his unwelcome announcement about the

40

station. During all the chaos, anyone could have fallen into the river and we'd have assumed they'd just moved on.'

Norman shook his head. 'I can't be sure, but I reckon if this man had died three months ago, he'd be in an even worse state. I reckon he died more recently than that.'

'In that case, we folks are the only ones that stayed and we're all here.'

Everyone stood in silence until Benny spoke up.

'But what about the people who come looking for the silver?' he said. 'More have come since silver coins have started washing up down by the falls.'

'It's dangerous down there,' Wyndham said with an embarrassed cough, 'but I always tell everyone to be careful.'

Wyndham looked at Seymour for support and he stepped forward.

'Wyndham's right,' he said. 'He told me about the dangers of getting too close to the water and he was planning to tell me where the safest routes to explore were. If this man came here to look for the silver and he slipped and fell into the water, that's his own fault.'

Wyndham smiled while Benny moved away from the bar to slap him on the shoulder.

'I didn't mean it that way,' he said. 'Nobody is blaming you.'

A ripple of nods and affirmative grunts passed

around the room, but Wyndham couldn't help but notice that Norman didn't join them in providing support. Instead, he peered at the wrapped-up body, as if he might still figure out more information. But with him not offering any further thoughts, the group turned to the practical matter of burying the body.

Everyone bustled as they allocated tasks and then disbanded. Wyndham didn't join in, figuring he'd done enough already and so, with Seymour, he headed to the bar where Seymour bought them both whiskeys.

'Obliged,' Wyndham said as he sipped his drink.

'Don't be,' Seymour said. 'I'm paying for the drinks with that dollar you dropped down by the water.'

Wyndham winced, but when he noticed that Seymour was smiling, he leaned towards him and sighed.

'Last month, I really did find a dollar while I was showing this visitor around. We were both so excited we spent two days combing the area, but we didn't find any more. The next week I took this other man down there and he wasn't impressed by what he saw. So I tried to liven up the search.'

'Did it work?'

'In the end, I guess it did. I couldn't feign my excitement very well so he wasn't impressed, but later someone arrived having heard about the money

42

washing up, and so I've kept doing it.' Wyndham considered Seymour. 'You're not annoyed, are you?'

Seymour removed the dollar from his pocket and tossed it on the bar.

'By the time we've drunk up your dollar I won't be.' He waited until Wyndham smiled and then gestured for Benny to fill their glasses. 'And I wasn't lying earlier. You planting the money is a better option than the strongbox having broken open.'

They sat quietly while a delegation returned to take care of the body. When they'd carried it away, with Norman following on behind and still looking thoughtful, Wyndham swirled his drink and shuffled closer to Seymour.

'I haven't deceived you about anything else. My best guess about what happened to the money is that it fetched up in the same place that the body came from.'

Seymour nodded. 'Because there's a calm area there?'

'Whether things end up there because the area is calm, or it's calm because things have ended up there and created a dam under the water, I don't know. But I do know that's where I'd look.'

'If you could get close enough without drowning.'

'There's the problem. Only dead men get to explore the water out there.'

'Which could be what the dead man was doing.'

'He could.' Wyndham looked aloft as an idea hit

him. He swirled round on his stool, but everyone had now left. 'Or then again he might be the cause of all this.'

He looked at Seymour until he returned an eager nod.

'Are you saying that man could be Kane Cresswell?'

'Nobody has ever found Kane's body.' Wyndham licked his lips as the idea took hold. 'But we might have finally done it.'

Seymour shrugged. 'I suppose that would solve a mystery, but that's no reason to get excited.'

'It sure is.' Wyndham winked at him. 'Because there might be a reward.'

'Who is he?' Sheriff Pollard asked as he came out of the law office.

'He's Herman Trask, a member of the Kane Cresswell gang,' Crosby Jensen said. Then, with a loud voice he dismissed Herman's dying taunt. 'In fact, he's the last one.'

'The last?' Pollard considered the body draped over Crosby's horse. 'US Marshal Lloyd Drake might disagree with you there.'

Crosby winced. 'Why?'

'The marshal came through town today. He was hot on the trail of someone from that gang. He wouldn't say who it was, but I'm sure it wasn't this man.'

Crosby frowned, but now that it looked certain that Herman hadn't been lying, the thought grew that after the relative ease with which he'd brought in the last two bandits he'd welcome the chance of finding another.

First though, he would have to get ahead of the marshal, and so he took the details of where the lawman had gone. Then he left town quickly.

The marshal had ridden out of Black Town several hours earlier, heading upriver towards Silver Falls, and he'd taken a route beside the Black River, letting Crosby follow him with ease.

He didn't expect to catch up with him before sundown, but as it turned out, four hours later when he approached the first building he'd come across, two men were outside.

The building beside the water was derelict, and the men were standing on a stretch of land close to the river. They were locked in an intense discussion but, as he was some distance away, Crosby couldn't tell what they were doing or if he'd caught up with the lawman.

Luckily, with their attentions being on each other, he was able to move on quickly and let the corner of the building hide him. Then he swung towards the building and dismounted a hundred yards away.

On foot he made his way to the nearest wall where he listened. The two men were talking, using low and tense tones, and now that he was here the thought came that he'd probably been mistaken.

He knew the marshal only by reputation, but if the lawman had tracked down another gang member, he'd have surely arrested him straight away. Crosby was planning how he'd move away without being noticed when a thud sounded on the other side of the building and the rickety structure shook, suggesting that someone had fallen against it.

Rapid footfalls sounded, but after only a few paces two quick gunshots tore out followed by a cry of pain. Crosby moved on to the corner of the building and when he peered round the side he saw the head and arms of a man lying on the ground.

The other man moved into view and stood over the body with his gun aimed down. The shot man was still, his posture suggesting he'd been killed, so the shooter slapped a hand on his shoulder aiming to drag him back behind the building, but then he saw Crosby.

The man swung his gun towards him, quickly forcing Crosby to jerk back out of view.

'What are you doing here?' the man called.

'I came to ask you the same question,' Crosby said with his back to the wall while drawing his gun. 'But I can see now what you're doing.'

'And what did you see?'

'I'm guessing you're US Marshal Lloyd Drake and you beat me to another member of the Kane Cresswell gang.'

Silence reigned for several moments.

'You guessed right. Who are you?'

'I'm a bounty hunter, Crosby Jensen. I thought I'd found the last member yesterday, but it seems I was wrong.'

Shuffling sounded as Drake moved the body, presumably giving him time to decide how to react to the situation.

'Come out into the open and tell me about the man you tracked down.'

Crosby figured he had no choice but to comply, so he lowered his gun and stepped out beyond the corner to find that a man with a star was already facing the corner. He was also holding his gun held low.

'I tracked Herman Trask for a month,' Crosby said, 'but he circled round, always staying close to Silver Falls. I finally caught up with him and left his body with Sheriff Pollard.'

The body had been dragged out of sight, but Crosby glanced at the corner and so Drake invited him to join him in moving around the building. As he'd expected, Crosby found that the man had been shot in the back, this probably being the reason for the lawman's pensive attitude.

Drake looked Crosby in the eye. 'I'm grateful you dealt with Herman, the last bandit gang-member.'

'But I'd heard. . . .' Crosby shrugged. 'Then who's this man?'

47

'Kane Cresswell had inside help. This man was a train guard.'

'I had wondered if that might be the case.' Crosby knelt down beside the body. 'So it doesn't surprise me that he resisted arrest and turned a concealed gun on you.'

Drake smiled. 'I'm pleased we understand each other.'

Crosby stood up. 'We do. This man got what he deserved. Being a bandit is bad, but being a guard and taking money to help the bandits is worse. If he'd done his duty, my friend Ewan Douglas might still be alive.'

'You could be right, and you weren't far wrong with your summary. I had intended to arrest him, but I gave him a chance to confess first. Instead, he fled and I had to stop him.' Drake moved over to the body and took his legs. 'But it'd be best if I didn't have to answer too many questions about his demise.'

When Drake glanced at the river, Crosby got his meaning, but he still shook his head.

'I could take him in and claim I shot him.'

'There'll be no reward for this one. Nobody else has worked out he was involved.'

Crosby nodded and he wasted no more time before taking the body's arms. They walked him over to the water and unceremoniously tossed him into the river.

The strong current soon claimed the body and then they watched it swirl away until a heavy wave took the body beneath the surface.

'Is there any more of his kind?' Crosby asked.

'Other railroad men have questions to answer, and there's the other important thing I have to do before I can deem my mission complete.'

Drake didn't explain and so Crosby pondered for a moment before brightening.

'You mean find the missing money?'

Drake smiled. 'That's right, and before he died, that man had an interesting story to tell about what's been happening in Silver Falls recently.'

CHAPTER 5

'I don't accept that,' Norman said after Wyndham had outlined his theory. 'I've taken another look at the body and he's been shot. Everybody said that Kane Cresswell only drowned.'

Norman looked around the assembled group, but nobody volunteered to confirm his finding.

The townsfolk had found a box in the stable. Now the body was packed away in the box and two men had been dispatched to dig a hole.

'Kane's body has never been found,' Wyndham said, struggling to think of anything he could say that would make his theory sound more convincing.

'That doesn't make it any more likely the dead man is him.' Norman raised a hand when Wyndham started to reply. 'And don't mention the possibility of a reward, because Finnegan Kelly will be even less impressed with us if we tell him we've found Kane's body and it's not him.'

Wyndham had been about to mention a reward and the possibility that they could curry favour with the railroad. So he lowered his head, making Norman grunt in triumph, but it was Seymour who spoke up.

'I don't know much about your problems,' he said, 'but it seems to me this town has already died, so there's not much that can happen that'll make your situation worse. But if this body is Kane's, it might make things better.'

Wyndham raised his head to find several people were nodding, although Norman was shaking his head.

'I know Finnegan Kelly,' Norman said. 'He blames us for what happened to the money and no mouldering corpse is going to make him reopen the station.'

'We're not saying it will,' Wyndham said, 'but he might be grateful enough to give us something.'

'He won't be grateful.'

Wyndham set his hands on his hips, Norman's repeated rejections now making his blood race.

'I've heard enough!' Wyndham snapped. 'I don't have to explain nothing to you. I say that man is Kane Cresswell and we should contact Finnegan Kelly.'

'I agree,' Benny said before Norman could respond.

Norman looked around for support, but when he didn't receive any, he waved a dismissive hand at everyone and turned away. With his head down and while muttering to himself, he stomped out of the stable.

Wyndham watched him leave and then stood back to let the others take the lead in deciding what to do next. As it turned out, his suggestion was popular and everyone was enthused with the thought that contacting the railroad would improve their situation.

'So,' Benny said, when everyone had spoken their mind, 'we'll bury the body for now and then get a message to Finnegan Kelly.'

'And that,' Wyndham said, 'will just leave us with the question of whether this man will turn out to be Kane Cresswell.'

Everyone shrugged. Then two men, Percy and Quincy, moved forward to take the box while everyone else turned to the door, but while they'd been talking two men had arrived quietly.

Wyndham's old friend Crosby Jensen had returned and he was standing in the stable doorway with another man who Wyndham didn't recognize.

'My new friend here might be able to help you with that,' Crosby said while directing a cheery nod at Wyndham.

'How can he do that?' Wyndham said.

Crosby stood aside and the other man stepped forward, letting everyone see the star on his chest.

'Because I'm the man who was tasked with rounding

up the Kane Cresswell gang,' he said. 'I'm US Marshal Lloyd Drake.'

In the silent stable Drake moved over to the box. Crosby stayed at the door while everyone watched Drake remove the lid and consider the body within.

'Is it him?' Wyndham asked, unable to keep his silence.

'He's been dead awhile and I only ever came across Kane the once.'

Drake placed the lid back on the box and turned to face everyone.

'So what can we tell the railroad?'

Drake rubbed his jaw as if thinking. Then a slow smile spread across his face.

'You can tell them,' he said, 'that Kane Cresswell is back in town.'

'Are you sure that was Kane?' Crosby asked when he and Drake reached the bottom of Silver Gorge.

'There wasn't much left,' Drake said, 'but I'm certain enough it was him to explain to the railroad when they arrive.'

Crosby nodded and then looked at the water at the spot where Wyndham had seen the body come to the surface. Crosby could see that even if the strong-box had fetched up in the same place, they wouldn't be able to reach it and so he moved on to consider the river that flowed away from the falls.

He walked for a hundred yards down the side of

the water before he returned to find that Drake was still staring at the water.

'Three months on,' he said, 'we're not going to find something that everyone who has come here has failed to spot. I'll enjoy some time with my old friend Wyndham, but then I'm moving on.'

'I didn't think you were a man who gave up that easily,' Drake said, still looking at the water.

'I got involved in this because I wanted to find the men who killed my friend. Now that I've done that, I have to think like a bounty hunter and weigh up the risks against the potential gain. Even if the risks are low this time, I can't see any way I'll gain.'

'Then you're wrong. The risks are high, but then again so is the potential reward.'

'The people in town are too depressed to cause trouble.'

'The railroad blamed the town for the raid and the town blamed the railroad, but I reckon they were both to blame. That means someone up there knows more than they've let on, and when Finnegan Kelly hears that Kane's body has washed up, he'll come to protect his own secrets.'

Crosby joined Drake in looking at the water.

'You could be right, but that sounds like a problem for a lawman, not a bounty hunter. I'm leaving, unless you give me the names of people with a bounty on their heads or tell me how we're going to find the missing silver.'

Drake grunted to himself, but he didn't offer anything and so Crosby turned away. He figured that after a night reminiscing with Wyndham about their time on the bridge, he'd carry out his promise tomorrow.

He sought out the path back up the side of the gorge, but he had moved for only a few steps when a gunshot rang out, the sound echoing in the confined space despite the roar of the water.

He didn't see where the shot landed and so he swirled round to find that Drake had crouched down while looking around as he sought out the location of the shooter. Then the marshal moved quickly for the nearest cover of a boulder lying beside the water.

Crosby followed him and a second shot rang out that clipped into the rock, ensuring that both men crouched down in the shallows.

'He's not much higher than we are,' Drake said, pointing up the gorge. 'Perhaps on the path back up.'

Crosby lowered Drake's hand to indicate a position nearer to ground level.

'Even better, I reckon he's close,' he said.

Drake narrowed his eyes and then gave a brief nod. He pointed to either side, silently giving Crosby directions and then without waiting for Crosby to agree he moved out from the boulder.

Crosby moved off and together they ran for the start of the slope with their heads down, aiming to approach the position Crosby had indicated from either side. They had halved the distance to the slope when Crosby saw a tangle of fallen tree trunks lying twenty yards up the slope.

The trees were to the side of the route they'd taken down, and he judged that this was the position from where the shooter had fired.

Drake must have reached the same conclusion as he moved for one end of the trunks. Crosby took the other, although he stayed back to cover Drake and let him reach the trunks first.

Drake kept his head lowered until he reached the trunks. Then he bobbed up and trained his gun on the other side.

For several seconds he held the pose before moving cautiously sideways to see more of the ground beyond the trunks. He shook his head and looked further afield.

Crosby caught his meaning and looked beyond the trunks. The shooter must have seen that they'd worked out he wasn't behind the trees as two rapid shots tore out, making both men go to ground.

When Crosby glanced up it was to see movement fifty yards above him as the shooter beat a hasty retreat. His form slipped in and out of rocks and behind trees, but Drake still loosed off a shot at the fleeing man before moving on to look beyond the trunks.

Crosby stilled his fire as he kept his gun trained on

the shooter, but the man kept moving. He couldn't see him clearly enough to be sure he'd recognize him again, but the man was moving quickly, so he must be familiar with the area.

'He was on his own,' Drake called as he made his way down the slope.

By now the shooter was most of the way to the top of the gorge so Crosby holstered his gun and moved on to join Drake.

'Someone clearly didn't like seeing a US marshal snooping around.'

Drake shrugged. 'You're assuming he was shooting at me.'

Crosby laughed. 'I've never done anything to make someone take shots at me.'

Drake nodded and then peered up the gorge, but the shooter didn't come back into sight.

'You staying now?' he asked after a while.

'Sure am,' Crosby said.

CHAPTER 6

The Station Saloon hadn't been so full in three months. Nearly all the townsfolk were here, along with the newcomers.

The townsfolk were in good spirits as they discussed Finnegan Kelly's likely response now that a message had been sent to the railroad, while the newcomer Seymour Banks sat with Wyndham and Crosby at a table in the corner.

They pored over a map Wyndham had made of the area to help Seymour plan where he would search tomorrow. Marshal Drake sat quietly eyeing the cheerful townsfolk with what Wyndham took to be suspicion.

When Drake noted he was looking at him, Wyndham sat back to let Crosby and Seymour exchange ideas while he returned to the novel he had been reading, losing himself in a story he'd read many times. He became so engrossed that the next time he looked up, he flinched on finding that Drake was still looking at him.

Wyndham acknowledged him with a smile and that encouraged Drake to come over.

'I gather you're the man with all the answers around here,' Drake said, sitting at their table.

'I work as a guide for anyone who wants to look for the silver,' Wyndham said.

Drake swirled the whiskey in his glass. 'What would you do if someone actually found it?'

'I hope I'd be with them when they did.' He glanced at Seymour, who provided a supportive grunt. 'If I wasn't, I'd move on and do something else, like Crosby has done. I don't want to spend the rest of my life taking people down to the falls.'

Crosby must have caught on that Drake was fishing for information as he slapped Wyndham on the back.

'Wyndham's an old and trusted friend,' he said. 'I reckon he could do anything he put his mind to.'

'Anything, you say?' Drake said.

Wyndham was about to provide a casual retort, but then decided to avoid alarming the lawman. He put down his book and, choosing his words carefully, he answered using a level tone, showing he had nothing to hide.

'I looked after the security for the bridge while it was being built, along with Crosby and five other men. We did a good job and hardly anything went missing.'

'Then a man with your talents could be useful to me.' Drake looked around the saloon. 'Is everyone that lives here in the saloon tonight?'

'Everyone but Norman Pierce.'

Drake looked aloft. 'I remember that name. He used to run the railroad office here.'

'He did,' Wyndham said, although he didn't think Drake had asked a question.

Drake smiled. 'So what can I do here while I wait for the railroad to arrive?'

Wyndham shrugged. 'Relax.'

Drake frowned and then turned Wyndham's book round so that he could read the title.

'*From the Earth to the Moon* by Jules Verne,' he said, and then drew the book closer to consider the cover, which showed a projectile hurtling towards the moon. 'I assume this is a story?'

'It is.'

'I've never been one for stories. I prefer to deal with reality.'

Wyndham nodded, but when Drake continued to look at the book cover, he leaned forward.

'I've read it before, so you can borrow it if you want.'

Drake didn't reply, but he did open the book. Wyndham exchanged a smile with Crosby and then, with Drake not appearing as if he would ask more questions, he looked at the door.

Seymour and Crosby both nodded and they joined

him in heading outside and then on to Wyndham's home on the outskirts of town. Wyndham had agreed earlier that Seymour could stay with him before he embarked on his search tomorrow while Crosby would stay with him for as long as he remained here.

He had no idea where Drake would rest up.

Seymour clearly had a plan in mind and Wyndham didn't question him about it, figuring that like most people who came in search of the silver, he wanted to keep his idea to himself.

In the morning, Crosby had no interest in seeing the river again and so he and Seymour set off early. Wyndham planned to guide Seymour on his trip downriver for as far as he could travel while ensuring he could get back by sundown.

Seymour was content with this arrangement and when they reached the top of the gorge he finally revealed his plans.

'When you showed me that quiet stretch of water, you got me thinking,' he said. 'I reckon the silver could have come to rest in a patch like that one, so that's what I intend to look for.'

'I agree,' Wyndham said as they made their way down the slope. 'But I still think the calm stretch beside the falls is the silver's most likely final resting-place.'

'It could be, but it's impossible to reach that place, so there's no point in worrying about it. I'd look for patches of calm water I can reach.'

'I'll show you the ones I know about and that should help you identify the areas where you might find more.'

Seymour smiled and then, after they'd made their way down the gorge for a few minutes, he slapped him on the back.

'I like the advice you've given. If I get lucky, I'll make sure you get something out of it, too.'

Nobody had ever made him such an offer, but before he could thank him, Wyndham noticed something on the edge of the water below. He came to a sudden halt, the scene appearing the same as it had done yesterday, making Seymour look at him oddly.

'A body,' Wyndham said, pointing.

Seymour turned back and then winced. 'There's more than one, this time.'

Wyndham narrowed his eyes, judging that Seymour was right, and so when they moved on, they did so with heavy treads.

Sure enough, when they reached the bottom of the gorge, two bodies were lying in the shallows, their forms rising and falling with the waves breaking on the shore.

They stopped beside a boulder to consider the scene. The bodies were lying twenty yards apart on their fronts and it may have been the similarity of the situation, but both the bodies felt familiar.

'Do you want to start your search without me?' Wyndham said after a while. 'Or do you want to try again tomorrow?'

'You'll need help to get them out of here, so I'll start looking after we've dealt with this. Besides, the way this is working out, more bodies could turn up tomorrow.'

'I hope not, but either way, this isn't our problem. We have a lawman in town, so he can deal with this.'

Seymour nodded. 'I'd heard that another one of the bandits followed Kane Cresswell into the water a few weeks after the raid, so one of the men could be him.'

They moved closer to the first body, confirming he was in as bad a state as Kane had been in, but when they moved on to the second body, Wyndham found out why the situation was making him uneasy.

He recognized the dead man.

'It's possible,' he said, 'but this one died more recently than that. It's Norman Pierce.'

'You reckon this man is our mystery shooter from yesterday?' Crosby asked when Wyndham and Seymour had left them to head downriver.

'I sure hope so,' Drake said, standing over the body. 'If not, I killed the wrong man.'

Crosby turned his back on Drake to cover his surprise and moved on to the second body. Like Kane Cresswell, this man had been in the water for some time.

He doubted anyone would be able to work out

who he was, but a flash of silver caught his eye. With his face averted so he didn't have to look at the body too closely, he patted the ragged clothing and entangled in the remnants was a silver watch.

He rubbed the slime away and examined it, finding the initials 'GW' on the back. The only person Crosby had ever met with those initials was his friend from the bridge, Gareth Wilson, which made him frown before he shook the worrying possibility away.

'This might help you to confirm who it is,' he said, holding out the watch.

Drake came over and took the watch. When he read the initials, he furrowed his brow and looked aloft, and so Crosby moved along the side of the water as he examined the area where Wyndham had claimed the bodies were coming from.

He didn't gather any ideas as to how this might help him find the silver and so he returned to Drake, who was leaning back against the boulder where they'd sought cover yesterday. He was turning the watch over in his hand while nodding to himself.

'The initials have confirmed who the body isn't,' Drake said when Crosby joined him. 'It's not the bandit who fell into the water.'

'Unless he stole the watch.'

'There's that possibility, but I reckon this is the second piece of evidence that points to the conspiracy that went on here.'

'So what is the conspiracy?' Crosby thought for a

moment. 'And what was the first piece?'

'The conspiracy concerns the railroad's attempt to cover up the details surrounding the loss of the silver. And the first piece of evidence is Norman Pierce, a man who used to work for the railroad.'

Crosby nodded. 'You reckon he was worried that you'd come here to expose that conspiracy and that's why he tried to shoot us up yesterday?'

'And why he was the only person in town who didn't come to the saloon last night.'

'So you tracked him down and killed him?'

'Sure.'

Crosby sighed. 'You sure are an unorthodox lawman.'

Drake tossed the watch up in the air and then slipped it in his pocket.

'I prefer to think that I'm effective,' he said. 'So what's the problem?'

'I've seen you track down two men who you reckon were involved in the raid and this conspiracy.' Crosby moved round to look at Norman's body. 'They were both shot in the back.'

'You're a bounty hunter. I'm sure you've done worse.'

'Herman Trask is the only man I've shot, and then my mission was to bring him in either dead or alive. You're a lawman and it's yet to be proven if either of those men did anything wrong. Worse, you're unlikely to get to the truth if you keep shooting men in the back.'

'I'll get to the truth when the railroad arrives to collect Kane's body.'

'How?'

'I don't who will come, but I do know that what they'll find here will provoke a reaction.' Drake smiled. 'You see, that body your friend Wyndham found yesterday wasn't Kane Cresswell's.'

'How will that. . . ?' Crosby shook his head, and then backed away for a pace while waving a dismissive hand at Drake. 'Don't answer that. I don't care about this any more. You're playing a dangerous game and none of this is my concern.'

Drake shrugged. 'You sounded interested yesterday.'

'That was when I thought we might find the silver, but you have no idea where it's ended up and what you're doing won't find it either.'

For long moments Drake considered him and then he conceded Crosby's point with a shrug.

'Go, then.'

Crosby backed away for several slow paces, giving Drake a chance to offer something that would make him stay, but when he said nothing else, he turned and headed for the slope. Behind him, Drake moved on to the bodies, but Crosby had no intention of helping him.

He had halved the distance to the slope when a powerful punch slammed into his back. His legs went numb and he dropped to his knees.

Through his befuddled senses he registered that he had heard a gunshot, but by then he was keeling over to lie on his chest. A mixture of pain and anger at himself for turning his back on Drake made him cry out in anguish.

A hand slapped down on his shoulder and rolled him over on to his back. Drake peered down at him, his form seemingly shrouded in mist.

'Why?' Crosby gasped.

'You might have talked about what I did and if I'm to uncover the truth, I can't have anyone knowing I'm here.'

'You're a lawman. Who would care that you're doing your duty?'

The long speech took Crosby's last remaining strength and he suffered the terrible feeling of slipping down into the soft ground. He shook away the feeling and found Drake smiling at him.

'Anyone who is smarter than you are would care because when they learn that the body isn't Kane Cresswell's they'll ask the question you didn't ask.'

Crosby wheezed in a long breath. 'I should have asked you whose body it is?'

Drake shook his head. 'Still the wrong question.'

Crosby tried to raise his head, but he couldn't move and he could no longer see Drake.

'Tell me,' he murmured.

'I'm not US Marshal Lloyd Drake. When you came

across us, I'd just killed him. I stole his star and took his identity.'

'Who are you?'

Crosby wasn't sure if he'd spoken aloud and when the answer came, it was if the speaker was standing at the end of a long tunnel.

'I didn't drown in the river. I got out and now I'm back to make everyone who wronged me pay.' He moved away, his voice becoming a faint breeze beyond the end of the tunnel. 'But before they die, I'll make sure they all know that I'm the man they couldn't kill – Kane Cresswell.'

CHAPTER 7

At sundown, the townsfolk were still acting in an animated manner when Wyndham arrived back in town.

He had taken Seymour several miles downriver while teaching him about the terrain and the vagaries of the current. Seymour had been grateful for his help and when he'd left him to continue his search, Seymour had been in good spirits.

On the return journey, Seymour's optimism didn't comfort Wyndham and he couldn't help but dwell on the events of the last two days. Even though two of the bodies were probably bandits and he'd never liked Norman, the situation made him uneasy.

He walked back by the falls to check that no more bodies had turned up while he'd been away. The shore was clear, but he reckoned he'd be checking more frequently from now on.

The townsfolk shared his pensive mood and he

received concerned glances from the people he passed. Then others gathered outside the stable to watch him approach while talking urgently.

'What's wrong?' Wyndham called out.

Dearborn Winters, the stable-owner, stepped forward.

'Another body has washed up,' he said. 'Same place, and in the same state as the others – except this time nobody has any idea who it is.'

Wyndham looked down as he considered who this new unfortunate might be. When he couldn't think of an explanation, he looked to the saloon.

'Is the marshal still in there?'

'Yeah, but he says he doesn't need to investigate this one.'

'Then we need to change his mind.'

With a nod to the gathered people he moved off. Dearborn and the others filed in behind him as he walked purposefully to the Station Saloon.

Inside, Drake was sitting at the same table he'd occupied last night.

Wyndham was amused to see that Drake was engrossed in reading the book he'd given him and didn't look up until he had reached his table. Then Drake considered him with irritation, before looking past him at Dearborn.

Drake raised an eyebrow and then put down the book, marking his place in the same way that Wyndham did by turning down a page.

'From the look of this delegation,' he said, 'you have a problem.'

'We do.' Dearborn gave a curt nod. 'Another unexplained body has turned up and we want to know what you intend to do about it.'

'I intend to find the guilty.'

Dearborn cast a significant glance at Drake's book and then looked around the saloon.

'How will you do that while sitting there reading?'

Drake narrowed his eyes, his stern gaze warning Dearborn not to question him again.

'Only a man like Wyndham who reads good books like this one will know how.' Drake glanced at the door. 'Leave us to talk about what we do next.'

Dearborn frowned but, after a few moments, he moved back a pace. With him relenting, the others joined him in backing away and then they left the saloon. Even Benny behind the bar busied himself elsewhere.

'So what do we do next?' Wyndham asked.

'I can only decide that when I've heard your side of the story,' Drake said.

'You'll have to make your decision first as I don't have a story to tell.'

Drake smiled and slapped the book. 'That's strange. You like a good story – both in telling them and reading them.'

Wyndham returned the smile and he relaxed enough to join Drake in sitting at the table.

'I can't help you explain where these bodies are coming from.'

'I reckon you can.' Drake leaned back in his chair and considered him. 'Which means the first thing I need to do is deputize you.'

' "Deputize" me?' Wyndham spluttered. 'Why in tarnation would you want to do that?'

'Because the train's due in two days and this time I reckon it'll stop. Someone from the railroad, presumably Finnegan Kelly, will be on board to collect Kane Cresswell's body and what he finds here will shake some answers out of him.'

'About what?'

'Three months ago something wrong happened here beyond just a failed train raid. I need help to work out what it was.'

Wyndham shrugged. 'Why not just use Crosby? He's a decent man – reliable, too.'

Drake frowned. 'Crosby decided to move on downriver, so I need someone else.'

Wyndham glanced away as he failed to hide his disappointment. He had thought Crosby would stay for a while and he hoped they might foster the camaraderie he'd enjoyed with Gareth and the others.

He had even thought that might encourage him to go in search of his old comrades. But perhaps he had to accept it was hard to rekindle old friendships when they had come together only because they happened to work together.

'I have no problem in helping you, but I have as little idea who the latest dead man is as everyone else has.'

Drake tapped a finger on the cover and raised it to begin reading again, but after a few words he looked up at him over the book.

'I don't need you to find an answer to that question,' he said. 'I know who the latest body to turn up is, along with the one this morning. I also know the body yesterday wasn't Kane Cresswell's.'

Drake waited until Wyndham's mouth fell open in surprise and then placed his book on the table face down. 'You can join me for a sense of duty, or for revenge. I don't care which.'

'Why revenge?'

Drake got up and beckoned Wyndham to follow. He headed outside. The townsfolk had dispersed, although Dearborn was still standing outside the stable watching the saloon.

When Dearborn saw them heading towards them, he moved aside. Drake shooed him further away before going inside. Three bodies were in a line along the back wall, the nearest being Norman's.

Drake stayed in the doorway, as Wyndham moved on to look the bodies over. He saw nothing that would help him identify the new one, and so he returned to Drake while shaking his head.

Watching him carefully, Drake withdrew a watch from his pocket.

'This was found on the body you came across this morning.'

Wyndham took the watch and turned it over to find the initials 'GW' on the back. He shrugged, but Drake's piercing gaze suggested that he should have gathered the significance.

He cast his mind back and with a start he thought of one person who had those initials. Then he gulped and he had to put a hand to the stable door to stop himself from stumbling.

He took a couple of deep breaths and then turned to Drake, hoping he'd explain what was on his mind and confirm that his assumption was wrong, but Drake just provided a sympathetic frown. Wyndham hurried back across the stable to stand over the bodies, searching for confirmation.

'My old friend Gareth Wilson – one of the men who looked after the bridge and railroad security – had a watch, but I never paid much attention to it.'

'And the other unidentified body?'

Wyndham gulped and this time the room seemed to swirl around him as the full horror of the situation hit him.

'Are you saying all three of the unidentified bodies are my friends?'

Drake slowly paced across the stable to stand beside him.

'I can't say that for sure, but I was hoping you'd be able to confirm it.'

'I can't. Aside from Crosby, I haven't seen them since they moved on three months ago and there's so little of them left.' Wyndham sighed. 'But they planned to look for work elsewhere, so there's no reason for them to wash up dead in the river.'

He looked at Drake, hoping he'd offer some encouragement, but the lawman shook his head.

'Whoever these people were, they were all shot and I want to know who did it.'

Wyndham looked again at the watch, trying to recall seeing Gareth using it, but the shock of this revelation had numbed his mind and he could recall nothing. Then he winced.

'You've never been here before and yet you worked out who they were.'

'I'm a lawman. It's my job to work things out and this discovery confirmed some of my suspicions. Finnegan Kelly had no reason to blame Silver Falls for the train raid and yet he did. That means the raid wasn't everything it seemed and when that happens, people who know too much can end up dead.'

Wyndham shook his head. 'That sure doesn't include my friends. We never had no trouble, and when the first train went over the bridge we were no longer guarding it because our duties had ended. Only Ewan was on board, and he went to enjoy the occasion, not to guard the train.'

Drake smiled, seemingly more pleased with that answer than Wyndham expected.

'That tells me most of everything I need to know before the railroad arrives. I'll get the rest of the answers out of them. You want to help me?'

Wyndham glanced at the bodies and now that he was thinking more calmly, he could believe two of them were the right height and build to be his friends.

'Sure,' he said.

CHAPTER 8

'Marvin Reynolds, Finnegan Kelly's hired gun, has come,' Wyndham said, peering through the saloon window. 'He has three men with him.'

'What are they doing?' Drake asked.

Wyndham looked over his shoulder to find that Drake was still sitting at the table reading his latest book. After he'd finished the last one, Wyndham had lent him another book by Jules Verne; this time *Twenty Thousand Leagues under the Sea.*

'It'd be easier if you just came over here and saw for yourself.'

'I will do.' Drake glanced up. 'But I've just got to an exciting part.'

Wyndham snorted a laugh, enjoying seeing how calm the lawman was being. For the last two days, as they'd waited for the next train, Wyndham had mainly stayed with Drake in the saloon brooding over whether the dead men were in fact his friends and, if they were, why they'd been killed.

He figured that he'd only accept it if more bodies washed up and so accounted for everyone who could have gone into the water, but this was also the last thing he wanted to happen. Accordingly, twice a day he'd gone into the gorge, but mercifully the shore had remained free of bodies.

He gathered no clues as to why Norman had been killed either, but now he hoped he might get answers about some of the mysteries as he watched Marvin go in search of answers of his own.

Marvin was one of the men who had been with Finnegan when he'd been run out of town, so presumably he knew whatever Finnegan knew. Dearborn Winters had greeted them and he was taking them down the main drag past the saloon.

'They're going to the stable,' Wyndham said.

'Why didn't you say so?' Drake said. He marked his page and slammed his book closed. 'I thought Marvin would come in here and see me first.'

He crossed the floor of the saloon and stood beside Wyndham to peer at the stable. The three men stayed outside and looked around while Dearborn took Marvin inside.

They were in the stable for only a few moments and when Dearborn came out he was clutching a spade, suggesting Marvin had given the bodies in there only a cursory glance.

He collected his three men and they all headed

behind the stable towards the spot where the man the townsfolk still thought was Kane had been buried.

'So he's only interested in Kane,' Wyndham said. 'Yet again the railroad didn't think my friends' deaths were important.'

'I think it's more likely that their deaths weren't a surprise and he wants to make it look as if they're not important.'

'You're saying he was involved in killing them?'

'That's my assumption, and in the next few minutes I'll prove that and hopefully find out why he did it.'

Wyndham didn't need any further encouragement and without Drake giving him any instructions he slipped through the door. The railroad men were moving from view and so he walked down the main drag.

He heard Drake following him, confirming that he was doing the right thing, but his anger kept him walking until he reached the stable where he'd calmed down enough to stop.

'What are your orders?' he asked quietly, his voice gruff.

'We split up and get as close to them as we can without being seen. Wait until I make the first move and then remember that these men killed your friends.'

Drake gave Wyndham a long look. While working

as a bridge guard Wyndham had always carried a gun and he'd been prepared to use it, but as it turned out, he'd never had to face any trouble.

This time, he felt ready to cause some trouble of his own and he patted his holster, making Drake nod. Then Drake hurried off down the main drag and slipped between two disused buildings.

Wyndham assumed he aimed to skirt around the town to reach a position beyond the fresh grave. So he took the shorter route by heading to the other side of the stable and hurrying along to the back corner.

When he peered around the corner, he faced the backs of the four railroad men who were standing in an arc to watch Dearborn dig. They were making no effort to help him, but the box was only a foot down and Dearborn had already uncovered most of the lid.

Dearborn scraped the last of the earth away and slipped the shovel under the lid, but Marvin raised a hand before he could lever it up and gestured for one of his men to complete the task. That man moved in and, with a firm, downwards thrust he prised the lid away, making it flip into the air and turn over before it thudded down.

Marvin moved in and peered down at the body. His eyes narrowed. Then he looked up at Dearborn.

'I knew I should never have come here again,' Marvin snarled. 'But now that I have, you people have annoyed me for the last time.'

Marvin shot a glance at his men and they moved towards Dearborn, who backed away a pace, cautiously.

'You mean that's not Kane?' he asked.

'Kane looked nothing like that.'

'How can you be so sure? You said you'd never seen him before.'

Marvin's eyes flared, making Dearborn wince, clearly accepting he'd made a mistake. Then the man holding the shovel advanced on him.

Dearborn raised an arm before his face as his opponent raised the shovel high, but before the man could swing it at him, Wyndham stepped forward.

'Leave him alone,' he demanded.

The men turned to face him, giving Dearborn a chance to scurry out of reach of the shovel. Marvin snorted with contempt when he recognized him.

'I should have realized you'd be involved in this,' he said. 'You didn't try to stop the bandits when Kane raided the train, and you've failed again.'

'I haven't "failed". I've already learnt one valuable piece of information: the railroad knew about Kane Cresswell before the raid and, like Dearborn said, back when Finnegan decided to close the station, he didn't tell us that.'

Marvin shrugged. 'I don't have to explain nothing to you.'

Wyndham glanced around, but he couldn't see Drake, or any sign of where he was undoubtedly watching this encounter. His instructions were to let Drake make the first move and although he'd failed to do that, he figured he shouldn't reveal that he was now a deputy marshal, which would suggest that Drake was here.

'This town died because of that raid, and now dead bodies have started washing up beyond the falls. We deserve to know what's going on.'

'The last people to learn what was going on ended up dead. Do you want to risk that?'

Marvin glanced at the stable with a subconscious gesture that told Wyndham who those 'last people' were. Wyndham set his feet wide apart and edged his hand towards his holster.

'As those people were my friends, tell me.'

Marvin frowned, seeming for a moment as if he would explain. Then he shook his head.

His men must have understood the gesture as one man threw the shovel to the ground while the other two men moved for their guns. Wyndham jerked his own hand towards his holster, but then he accepted he stood no chance of prevailing against three gunmen.

He stayed his hand and threw himself to the side. He had been standing three paces beyond the corner of the stable and now that short distance felt like it was three hundred paces as, from the corner of his eye, he saw the three gunmen drawing their guns.

With his head thrust down, he leapt behind cover.

He moved so quickly that he barrelled into the wall, shoulder first, making the wall rattle.

He stood upright, gulping in relief that the gunmen hadn't fired, but then footfalls thudded as the gunmen approached. In a rush, he turned towards the front of the stable and set off at a sprint, the short journey to the main drag again feeling many times longer than its actual length.

He'd covered half the distance before gunfire rattled behind him, making him duck, but he was able to run on. He managed two more paces, but then the difficulty of running quickly while doubled over became too demanding and he stumbled before going to his knees.

His shoulder hit the ground and he tipped over, somersaulting once before again landing on his knees. He was close enough to reach out and touch the corner and so, abandoning any attempt to effect a dignified departure, he scrambled on hands and feet around to the front of the stable.

A sharp burst of gunfire sounded, followed by a pained screech. For the first time the thought hit Wyndham that he might not be the gunmen's primary target and he leapt to his feet.

When he looked around the corner it was to see Dearborn facing him with the gunmen lined up behind him. Dearborn met Wyndham's eye before he keeled over on to his chest to reveal a bloodied back.

Dearborn didn't move again and so the gunmen turned to face Wyndham, making him jerk back out of sight where he pressed his back to the wall. Further into town the gunfire had encouraged the townsfolk to edge out on to the main drag, from where Wyndham shooed them away.

'Marvin Reynolds shot up Dearborn,' he shouted when nobody heeded his warning. 'We're next!'

Wyndham didn't know this for sure, but his statement produced the desired effect when everyone moved back out of sight. Wyndham reckoned he should join them and he looked for the furthest building he could reach before the gunmen arrived.

He chose the saloon and set off at a sprint, but this time he drew his gun. When he reached the centre of the main drag he glanced over his shoulder.

The gunmen hadn't appeared yet, so he ran on with a sideways shuffling gait that let him look backwards while still covering ground quickly.

He reached the saloon without incident so he slowed to a halt. Benny Stokes was lurking in the shadows and he hurried on to the doorway.

'Why did Marvin kill Dearborn?' he asked.

'The body wasn't Kane Cresswell's,' Wyndham said. He stood on the boardwalk and looked down the main drag to the stable. 'But I don't reckon he killed him out of anger. He's protecting his own secrets – except I'm not sure what they are yet.'

'With the look of things, I doubt we'll find out the

truth, but he'll come after the rest of us next.' Benny sighed. 'At least we have a US marshal on our side.'

'It didn't help Dearborn none,' Wyndham said as Benny hurried across the saloon, presumably to collect a weapon.

Wyndham looked for signs of where Drake had gone to ground, but he failed to see him and worse – Marvin led the gunmen out on to the main drag. Wyndham raised his gun, but the gunmen sidled quickly through the stable door.

A few moments later one man looked through the doorway and aimed at the saloon while two other men came running out. Wyndham followed them with his gun as they ran across the main drag, but he'd yet to get them in his sights when the gunman in the saloon fired, winging a shot into the saloon door.

Wyndham flinched away. Then, choosing discretion, he slipped into the saloon while another shot hurried him on his way. When he looked out, the men had all slipped from view.

'I assume they're coming for us,' Benny said, hurrying across the saloon with a rifle in hand.

Wyndham nodded. 'I reckon two men are making their way down this side of the main drag and another gunman is covering them from the stable.'

'Marvin is a fearsome gunslinger, but not the others. So I reckon our best chance is to make sure we get him.'

'He knows that. That's why he's staying in the stable and besides, I reckon he's the only one here with answers.'

Benny shrugged. 'I'd sooner be alive and remain confused than be dead and informed.'

Wyndham accepted Benny's point with a grunt. Then he moved to one side of the door while directing Benny to stand beside the window.

'You look out for the gunmen, and I'll watch the stable,' he said.

'Sure, Deputy Shelford.'

Benny caught Wyndham's eye and smiled: for the first time he had acknowledged Wyndham's status. Then they turned to the serious business of defending the saloon, but as it turned out the next movement they saw out on the main drag came from other townsfolk.

Six men emerged from hiding, presumably judging that they would be safer together rather than waiting for Marvin's gunmen to pick them off one by one.

Inside the saloon, Benny broke a window and laid down covering gunfire, although the gunmen weren't visible, and so Wyndham slipped outside.

'Get in here – quick!' he urged as he joined Benny in blasting lead down the main drag, although he was aiming at the stable.

Their steady gunfire ensured that the gunmen didn't show themselves. The running townsfolk were drawing level with the saloon and he was starting to think they would all reach safety when a feeling that something was wrong hit him.

The gunmen had been skilled and well organized, so they ought to be putting up more of a fight. He hadn't seen where they'd gone to ground, so he turned on the spot, wondering if they'd moved on.

He was still looking around when his concern was proved valid in the worst possible way. Gunfire tore out.

The sounds were rapid and seemingly coming from all directions, but he figured some of the shots had been fired from the other side of the saloon.

As a running man went down clutching his side, he accepted the gunmen must have scurried around the back of the saloon. By then it was too late to stop the rest of the townsfolk from running past the gap between the saloon and the next building.

Another man went down while the others skidded to a halt and looked beside the saloon. Caught in a moment of confusion, they wavered between continuing on towards the saloon and doubling back.

Before the gunmen could make them pay for their indecision, Wyndham ran along the front of the saloon and, with no consideration of his own safety, he swung out into clear space.

With his feet planted wide apart he picked out the nearest gunman. This man was in the process of shooting at one of the townsfolk, but Wyndham's arrival made him fire quickly and then jerk his gun round towards him.

Two gunshots rang out with Wyndham's shot slamming into the gunman's chest, felling him while the gunman's hastily aimed shot clattered into the saloon wall. The second gunslinger didn't register Wyndham's presence as he continued trying to pick off the townsfolk.

With grim determination he tore out another shot before Wyndham got him in his sights and hammered a shot into his stomach, making him double over. A second shot to the head downed him.

Then Wyndham swung round to consider the fallen and the result was as bad as he'd feared. Three people had been downed, and none of them was moving.

Benny made his cautious way out of the saloon to join him. While keeping one eye on the stable, he considered the bodies.

'It's a pity,' Benny said, his voice gruff, 'that your first mission as a deputy marshal couldn't have gone better.'

Wyndham winced, Benny's comment reminding him of his other concern that he'd put from his mind.

'Which just begs the question,' he muttered, 'where in tarnation is Marshal Drake?'

CHAPTER 9

Wyndham beckoned Benny to check on the fallen townsfolk while he reloaded. Then he moved on down the main drag towards the stable.

For most of the gunfight either he or Benny had watched the building and so he judged that Marvin and the surviving gunman should still be in there. He kept his gun trained on the doorway as he swung round to let the interior come into view.

He drew level with the stable and could see inside to the back wall before he got a hint of what was happening inside. He saw the feet of someone lying on the ground beyond the doorway and when he'd walked for a few more paces he confirmed that it was the last gunman, and he'd been shot.

Wyndham cast his mind back, but he couldn't recall the lucky shot that had dispatched this man. Besides, the man was lying several yards away from the doorway.

Then he remembered that when the gunmen had been shooting up the townsfolk, he'd heard gunfire from several directions – and perhaps not all of it had come from the gunmen and Benny.

'Marshal Drake,' he muttered to himself as he walked purposefully towards the stable.

Sure enough, when he reached the doorway Drake came into view. He was standing over Marvin Reynolds, who was lying on his back clutching a bloodied stomach while gasping in pain.

Drake cast Wyndham an unconcerned sideways glance as if he'd expected him, and pointed at Marvin.

'He's got a story to tell,' he said. 'Make sure you hear it before he breathes his last.'

'If it's about why he tried to destroy this town, I'm not interested,' Wyndham snapped. 'He succeeded. It looks like only five of us have survived, and that includes Benny Stokes and me.'

Drake continued to glare at the writhing Marvin, his gun held on him in case he gathered enough strength to fight back.

'Don't blame me for that. I came here to get answers, not to defend you folk.'

'That must be a comfort to you, otherwise you'd have failed in your mission.'

Drake's expression remained impassive and he didn't register that his words had annoyed him. He moved round Marvin, who watched him through pained eyes.

'This town deserved to die,' Marvin muttered through clenched teeth. 'And you won't get away with this.'

Drake snarled and raised his gun to sight Marvin's chest, forcing Wyndham to move in and brush his gun arm aside.

'Won't get away with what?' he demanded.

For several moments Marvin looked at Drake past Wyndham's shoulder before he let his head loll to the side to consider him. He snorted a laugh, the action making blood dribble out of the corner of his mouth.

'You'll find out in the end.' He laughed again, making his face contort in pain. 'I've heard the expression of getting the last laugh, but I never expected to experience it.'

With that defiant comment the fight appeared to go out of him. His hand slipped off his stomach to drop to the ground while his chuckling subsided to a gurgle in the back of his throat.

Wyndham stood over him and tapped a foot against his side until Marvin stopped laughing.

'You'll explain what you're finding funny, or somehow I'll keep you alive just so I can kill you all over again.'

'Finnegan Kelly killed the other bridge guards,' Marvin whispered, his voice so low that Wyndham had to lean over him. 'And you won't live for long

91

enough to work out why.'

He continued to murmur, but the words became too quiet and garbled for Wyndham to understand what he was saying. He shook him, but that only made Marvin become silent.

Presently, his breathing, too, was silenced. Wyndham looked up at Drake.

'You get what you wanted out of this?' he asked.

'Sure,' Drake said. 'But I'm sorry that you won't.'

Wyndham shrugged as he stood up straight and then walked up to Drake.

'Don't be so sure of that,' he said.

With a grunt of anger he swung a round-armed punch at Drake's face, but even though Drake was still watching Marvin, the marshal raised his gun arm, deflecting the blow. Then he thudded a short-armed punch into Wyndham's stomach that made Wyndham drop to his knees while coughing and gasping for air.

By the time he'd got his breath back, Drake had moved on to the doorway where he considered him benignly.

'You coming, Deputy?' he asked.

Wyndham sighed and got to his feet while rubbing his stomach.

'I guess I am. What's your orders now?'

Drake gestured at the man lying near the doorway and so Wyndham moved over to him. To his surprise this man was still breathing, so he dragged him to the side of the door and propped him up.

His ministrations made the man stir. He groaned and felt his wounded side. Wyndham batted his hand away and examined the man, finding that he'd suffered a nasty scrape across the side that had probably busted a rib.

The man didn't have a slug in him and he'd banged his head when he'd fallen, but Wyndham reckoned he'd live and so he stood aside to let Drake question him. Drake loomed over the man and dragged him to his feet to stand him up against the wall.

The man whimpered in pain and he struggled to stay upright, but Drake held him tightly until the man met his gaze.

'Finnegan Kelly sent you here to deal with me,' Drake said. 'You failed, but you got lucky. I'm letting you live. You get a horse, water, food and bandages, and in return you'll get a message to Finnegan.'

'What's the message?' the man asked, his voice gaining strength as he appeared to accept that he wasn't about to be killed.

'Tell him,' Drake said, 'I know where the silver is.'

'To the fallen,' Benny said, raising his whiskey glass.

'To them all,' Wyndham added, downing his whiskey.

'And may Marvin Reynolds rot in hell.'

'And may Finnegan Kelly join him there.'

The other three surviving members of the town, Percy, Quincy and Randolph, murmured in agreement before downing their whiskeys.

They hadn't invited Drake to join them in the salute, but then again he'd returned to his usual table where he had resumed reading his book. He was now sitting crouched over with an intense expression as if the gun battle had never happened and the story before him was the only thing that mattered.

Drake hadn't offered to help them take the bodies to the stable and, with the day almost over, they had delayed burying everyone until tomorrow. Even with Marvin dead, Wyndham wanted to uncover the full truth about the conspiracy, although right now the death of half of the town had numbed him.

Now that he had time to think, he recalled that the shack in which he and his friends had sat in the evenings to watch the bridge had burned down shortly after the raid.

At the time he had thought this an accident or perhaps his friends' high spirits before they left, but now he reckoned it fitted in with what had just happened here.

Finnegan had paid them off on the morning of the raid. He and Crosby had gone to town, and the others had stayed at the shack to watch the first train go over the bridge. But then Finnegan had got word to them about the free liquor, and they'd left.

Gareth had drawn attention to himself by mentioning the bandits riding out of town and so, when they returned to the shack, Finnegan had been worried they'd work out that he'd been involved. He'd killed Gareth and the others to preserve his secret.

That still left plenty of questions unanswered and so, with a glass in hand, he went over to Drake. He stood over him and waited until Drake had studiously completed his current page.

'Captain Nemo still has a few more leagues to go,' Drake said.

'And I assume this isn't over for us, either?' Wyndham asked.

Drake signified that Wyndham should sit and then marked his place.

'Marvin was involved with what happened here, but he wasn't responsible,' he said. 'Finnegan Kelly was behind everything and once he gets my message, he'll come, probably in force.'

'The next train is in four days and that's long enough even for an injured man to reach Finnegan.' Wyndham sighed. 'And I'll be here with you waiting for him.'

'I'm pleased to hear that, but the truth might be hard for you to take.' Drake offered a sympathetic frown. 'Are you sure you want to help me solve the mystery of Silver Falls?'

Wyndham slammed a fist on the table, making the book bounce and then topple over on to the floor.

'You will accept my help, or I'll . . . I'll take back my book and I won't let you borrow any others.'

Drake laughed as he rescued the book. 'I'm pleased you've regained your good humour. You'll need it. The fact that Finnegan killed your friends isn't as shocking as the full story of what happened here.'

Wyndham took a deep breath. 'I need to know.'

Drake frowned. 'Then I'm sorry to tell you that everything you and your friends did here, and which you're so proud about, meant nothing.'

Wyndham frowned. 'We guarded the bridge and we never faced no trouble.'

'There's a reason for that.' Drake leaned forward. 'Finnegan hired you to deal with trouble and, as it turned out, the man he had to fear was Kane Cresswell. He was a protection man, of the kind that makes sure your property doesn't come to harm – but only if you pay him what he wants.'

'We knew about plenty of sources of trouble, but Finnegan never mentioned him.'

'That's because Finnegan did a deal. Kane wouldn't cause any trouble, and he'd see off anyone who might cause Finnegan trouble. Kane did his job well because you had a quiet time.'

Wyndham lowered his head, accepting Drake's statement that the truth was tough to hear. He would no longer be able to recall with pleasure the nights they'd sat in the shack sharing liquor and lively stories while feeling pleased with themselves for doing a good job.

They hadn't done a good job. They were just looking as if they were being effective while someone else took care of protecting the bridge.

'Why did Kane raid the train?'

'Once the bridge had been built, Finnegan had to complete his side of the bargain and pay off Kane. Finnegan had done the deal without the permission of his bosses and so he had to raise the money somehow.'

Wyndham winced. 'So they hatched a plan to stage a raid.'

Drake nodded. 'Except it's worse than that. The train guards were in on the plan, and your friends were enticed away from the bridge. Then Finnegan gathered everyone in town for a celebration to make the situation look genuine.'

'Why is that worse?'

'Your friends were killed because Finnegan feared they'd work out that they'd been lured away. But, from what you've said, it seems they weren't concerned, so they died to protect a secret they weren't even aware of.'

Wyndham lowered his head. He wanted to refute the theory, but now that it'd been uttered, he knew it to be correct.

'I assume your boast to Finnegan that you know where the silver is now, is a ruse to get him here?'

'It's not. I now have an able deputy who knows the river and who has good ideas about where the silver could have fetched up.'

Wyndham coughed and rubbed his forehead as he tried, after the shocking revelations, to gather enthusiasm to discuss a mystery that had preoccupied him for the last three months.

'I believe the silver is in the calm stretch of water where the bodies washed up, but the water only looks calm on the surface. Beneath, the water is deep and wild.'

Drake laughed and raised the book. ' "Deep and wild" it may be, but I don't reckon it's as fearsome as the maelstrom in this story.'

'The maelstrom is only in a story. The reality is more fearsome. We'll never find a way to get to the silver, if that's where it is.'

'We might not, but Captain Nemo would be able to reach it.'

Wyndham mustered a supportive laugh, but then he noted the lively gleam in Drake's eye.

'You sound as if you're being serious.'

'I am, and that's your fault. You gave me this book to read and it's given me plenty to think about. Visiting the moon was clearly a ridiculous idea, but travelling underwater isn't.'

Wyndham snorted. 'So you reckon you could build a craft that could go underwater and find the silver?'

'I do.'

Wyndham narrowed his eyes and when Drake returned his gaze calmly, he leaned back in his chair while sighing.

'I should point out that in the book, Captain Nemo dies in the maelstrom.'

'Thank you for spoiling the ending for me.' Drake waved the book at him. 'But as you said earlier: Captain Nemo may die, but that's only in a story.'

CHAPTER 10

'There's our *Nautilus*,' Drake said, pointing at the mouldering remnants of an old, abandoned passenger car.

'That car wasn't deemed intact enough to travel on land any more,' Wyndham said. 'It sure as hell won't be good enough to do anything in the water.'

'Except sink,' Benny added.

The other townsfolk grunted their support of this opinion, but it didn't deter Drake. After the surviving townsfolk had buried the fallen this morning, Drake had insisted that everyone head to the bridge.

Wyndham had hoped that overnight Drake would have forgotten his idea or admitted he had been joking, but instead Drake had finished the book and had gained even more enthusiasm for his scheme.

After the bridge had been completed, unwanted and broken material had been left strewn around the town-side of the river. With his book tucked under an arm, Drake had paraded around the residue until he'd found several substantial pieces of debris.

He'd rejected a rusting locomotive as being too heavy and a cab as being too small, but he approved of the passenger car. It was about twenty paces long, and the wheels had been taken away, leaving just the body.

'I hope it will sink,' he said, slapping Benny on the back while smiling. 'Because that's what it's supposed to do.'

'Why?'

'Read the book and you'll find out.' Drake waved his book at him.

When Benny eyed the book with dismay, Wyndham stepped forward.

'Our marshal,' he said, 'reckons he can build a craft that will let him live under water for long enough to find the silver.'

'Nobody could do that,' Benny said, 'especially using that car.'

Benny flinched, seemingly only then noticing that he was casting doubt on the marshal, but Drake didn't appear too concerned.

'I agree,' he said, 'but you're judging it on its current state. Once you've finished your work, it'll be fit to live in.'

'My work?' Benny spluttered.

'I gather that before you tended bar you were a builder for the railroad, and you built your saloon with your own hands.'

'I've built plenty of things.' Benny waited until Drake nodded with approval. Then he waved his arms as he struggled to encapsulate all the things that were wrong about this scheme until with a sigh he settled for the simplest explanation of why this would fail. 'But I've never built anything like this before and I don't know how.'

Drake waved the book at him again.

'Everything you need to know is in here. Just follow the instructions and in a few days the *Nautilus* will be ready to go.'

Benny took the book and opened it up. He raised his eyebrows, clearly having expected to find diagrams and instructions. Then, with his brow furrowed, he found a pile of discarded planks to sit on so he could start reading.

Benny wouldn't get a single clue from the book on how he could build Captain Nemo's *Nautilus*, but Wyndham kept that thought to himself, figuring that while he was reading he wasn't wasting his time on Drake's doomed scheme.

Drake instructed the others to look for things they could use, without explaining what exactly he expected them to find, and then moved on through the discarded debris.

Even though he reckoned they stood no chance of succeeding, Wyndham had more of an idea of what might work than anyone else had and so he joined

Drake. He pointed out another abandoned car that had intact glass along with planks that could be used to strengthen the car and cover holes.

'Our first big problem,' he said after a while, 'is getting all this stuff back to town and then down into Silver Gorge.'

'Moving all this *will* take time,' Drake said. 'But I'm pleased that one person believes in my plan. Unless, of course, you're just humouring me.'

'It's the duty of a deputy to carry out the orders of his boss.'

'I'd prefer you to do this because you believe it'll work.'

Wyndham stopped looking for items and swung round to face Drake.

'I believe that a craft that travels underwater of the kind that Jules Verne described could be built, just as I believe it may even be possible to build a craft to go to the moon. But I don't believe we can build it.'

'I've found that people can do anything, if they're motivated, and fifty thousand dollars' worth of silver is plenty of motivation.'

'The railroad never posted a reward and even if they did, I doubt anyone wants to hand over the money to Finnegan Kelly when he arrives.'

Drake licked his lips. 'The railroad don't need to know.'

Wyndham flinched back in surprise. 'Are you

suggesting we keep the money, if we find it?'

'I'm suggesting my mission was to track down the Kane Cresswell gang, and that moved me on to solving the mystery of Silver Falls. I want to find the silver, but that doesn't mean I have to return all of it to its rightful owners.'

'You're not like any lawman I've ever met,' Wyndham murmured, aghast.

'You're right.' Drake set his hands on his hips. 'Now will that motivate you to believe we can make our very own *Nautilus*?'

'No. There's no way we can build a real *Nautilus*.' Wyndham considered Drake's stern posture and then sighed. 'But that doesn't mean we can't try.'

'This is where our trying ends,' Benny said.

He looked at Wyndham for support, and Wyndham had to nod.

'I know the route down into Silver Gorge better than anyone,' he said. 'And I can't see any way we'll get the car down there.'

With that pronouncement everyone turned to Drake, presuming this was the moment when his scheme finally died, but as he had done throughout the day he simply provided an amused expression.

It seemed that every complaint and setback only encouraged him more.

They had roped up the car and dragged it away from the place where it had been feeding termites for the last year. Getting the car to move for the first time had made it creak so much Wyndham had thought Drake would then admit he wouldn't risk his life going underwater in it.

Undaunted, Drake had led the team with enthusiasm on the trip back to town and then to the top of Silver Gorge. Here, Drake had called a halt with the car standing on the edge of the long slope down to the falls.

'I never said this would be easy,' Drake said. 'We'll face plenty of problems and this is another problem that needs a solution.'

'Any solution will be too great a risk. The car could roll the wrong way and kill the horses, or us.'

Drake shook his head. In irritation Wyndham kicked the side of the car. His foot landed with a resounding thud and the car must have been more precariously placed than he'd expected as it shifted position.

Wyndham hurried away, but after swinging towards him, the car lurched the other way. Then, with much creaking and amidst a rising cloud of dust, the car toppled over the edge.

Everyone rushed forward to see the car rolling on down the slope. The area at the top of the slope lacked trees and so with nothing to halt its progress the car continued to turn over with stately grace.

After every turn Wyndham expected it to shudder to a halt, but the slope was just steep enough to ensure it kept moving. He counted four revolutions before it reached the treeline, where the end slammed into a tall pine.

A loud crack sounded that could have come from the tree or the car, and that made the car swing round so that its front aimed down the slope. Then it toppled over, going end over end twice, skipping up into the air on the second revolution before crunching down.

This movement landed the car on the well-worn trail down into the gorge and so it then proceeded to slide down the slope. When it disappeared behind the trees, Wyndham could still hear its progress as the car ploughed down into the gorge, and he judged that it was showing no sign of slowing down.

Drake moved away from the edge to face him.

'That's one way of getting it down there,' he said.

With that, Wyndham and Drake headed down into the gorge, following the path the car had beaten, leaving the others to head back to the bridge to collect the next delivery.

When he reached the bottom, Wyndham saw that the car had stopped a dozen yards away from the water. Even better, despite the many broken planks, it had broadly kept its shape.

They stood to one side of the car looking at the water and Wyndham tried to imagine it slipping down into the water. Now that they were in the right place, he found this easy to do.

Unfortunately, he couldn't imagine the car emerging from the water.

'We're the only people here,' he said. 'And we've got another hour before the next load arrives, so you can tell me the truth. Do you reckon this will work?'

'It will,' Drake said. He nodded as he looked from the car to the water and back again with a look that suggested he was doing what Wyndham was doing and imagining the likely result of their efforts.

'And you'll go down there?'

'Sure.' Drake turned to him. 'I want my deputy to be with me and that means you need to believe it can work, too.'

'You keep on telling me to believe and I keep on trying, but even the thought of claiming the silver down there isn't motivating me to risk my life. I'd have as much chance of success if I swam out there and dived down. In other words, none.'

'You said you'd never get this car down here, but you did.'

Wyndham took a deep breath and moved on to the water's edge. When Drake joined him, he pointed at the calm stretch of water.

'So you reckon we can make the *Nautilus* waterproof. Then, with an engine powering us on, we'll glide under the water, find the silver, and return to the surface?'

Drake laughed. 'You've clearly been reading too many stories. If you tried that, you'd surely drown.'

'Then what are we doing?' Wyndham spluttered.

'As I told you, you have to believe we can do this. When you do that, you'll find a way to make it work. I had no idea how we could do this until I was standing here.' Drake raised a finger. 'But I do now.'

'Then help me to believe. Explain.'

Drake drew Wyndham closer and gestured at the shallow water.

'The river water under the bridge is as wild as it is here, and yet they built a bridge across it. There's plenty of wood left beside the bridge, so there's no reason why we can't build a smaller version down here.'

'There is. The men who built the bridge knew what they were doing.'

Drake shot Wyndham an aggrieved look, but when he saw that he was smiling he returned a smile.

'We don't need to overstretch ourselves. We build for as far as is safe.' He signified a spot a couple of dozen yards into the water where the bottom was still visible. 'Then we attach ropes to the *Nautilus* and drag it out on to our platform.'

'I may have shoved the car down the slope with a single kick, but there's no way we could drag it. For a start, whoever was pulling the car would have to be standing further out into the water to get it to the end of the platform.'

'They would, indeed.'

Wyndham considered Drake's knowing smile and

then turned to the water. He pointed across the river.

'We could build another platform on the other side of the water and with rope stretched across the river we could drag *Nautilus* on to the platform.'

'You see, when you start believing, you start working out how we can make this happen.'

Wyndham nodded. 'I can see it working that far, but when we dragged *Nautilus* off the edge of the platform, it'd probably float away, not sink.'

'We'll reinforce the base with any metal we can find and that'll make it heavy enough to sink.'

'Which, of course, is even worse. We'll drown!'

'Not if we can stop water getting in. Then, we can search down there for a while until we're ready to be dragged out of the water. After that, we can try again somewhere else.'

'I guess that might work,' Wyndham murmured, reluctantly.

Drake slapped him on the back. 'So, I'll ask you again: do you believe we can do this?'

CHAPTER 11

'So, do you believe this will work?' Benny Stokes asked when everyone had settled down in the Station Saloon for the evening.

'Sure,' Wyndham said. He swirled his glass of water while checking that Drake wasn't paying attention to them. 'If we had another month.'

'Except we don't have another month.'

Wyndham frowned, wondering if Finnegan would respond quickly to Drake's ultimatum and so be on board the train the next day.

The last three days had been a busy time, but it had been surprisingly rewarding.

Once Drake had explained his less ambitious plan, everyone's scepticism had receded somewhat. Then the townsfolk started to plan properly and everyone used whatever skills they possessed to help the project.

Percy and Quincy had worked on the bridge and

so they built the platforms on both sides of the water. Randolph had been in charge of raising and lowering equipment and he found several abandoned pulleys that he set about repairing.

Benny worked on making the car waterproof. He boarded over every window except for the one at the front, figuring that provided the best combination of security and the ability to see out.

When he wasn't supervising everyone, Drake found a boiler plate, which he used to officially name the craft *Nautilus*.

This left only Wyndham struggling to make a contribution. As he figured that his knowledge of the vagaries of the current was all he could offer, he worked on casting a rope across the river.

This task turned out to be easier than he'd expected. He went downriver from the falls for a couple of hundred yards where at a bend in the river he went out on a headland and secured one end of the rope while casting the other end into the water.

The current dragged the rope on, settling into a position a third of the way from the other side. Once the rope had played out to its full extent, another bend let the other end come to rest in a tangle of fallen trees.

It had then taken Wyndham several hours to work his way back to the bridge and down the other side to secure the other end. Then it'd taken him and Benny most of the next day to manoeuvre the rope

111

back upriver.

His ingenuity had delighted Drake and, as he had done after every success, he had asked him to confirm that he believed this scheme would work.

Wyndham had complied and now that the *Nautilus* was almost complete and the winching mechanism was in place, he found it even easier to believe.

Tonight, like every night, the townsfolk rested up in the saloon to discuss what they'd done that day and what they'd do the next day, while Drake sat on his own, reading. He was currently taking a journey to the centre of the earth, as Wyndham figured this story would be the least likely to give him any new ideas.

'I'm not sure now if it matters whether we get enough time to finish this before Finnegan Kelly arrives,' Wyndham said as he considered the animated conversations going on around them in the saloon. 'Everyone is more enthused than they've ever been since the station closed down.'

'They are, but that enthusiasm will die out quickly enough if the marshal can't deal with Finnegan, or if the *Nautilus* fails.'

'That could happen, but only if we let it.' Wyndham leaned over the bar. 'Drake has been right about one thing. If you believe you can do something, you'll find a way to do it. So we just have to believe we can make this town live again.'

Benny jutted his jaw and then shrugged.

'I guess it's hard to see past Finnegan's return, but after that, anything could be possible.'

With this positive thought cheering him, Wyndham left the saloon, figuring that tomorrow would be a long day and he would need all the rest he could get.

Sure enough, activity outside woke him at first light as everyone made full use of the available time.

The train was due in late afternoon and Drake was assuming that Finnegan would be on it. Wyndham reckoned that would give them enough time for one attempt.

Despite the urgency of acting quickly, with the *Nautilus* ready, Drake became cautious for the first time. He would be risking his life and so he started to systematically check every aspect of the procedure.

He got Randolph to check the pulley worked by dragging a log out on to the water past the calm patch of water. Then they dragged it back.

This worked without a hitch, although the log was roughly buffeted, suggesting the passage wouldn't be smooth. Then he dragged every log he could find on to the platform, and he even jumped up and down heavily, but the platform coped with the weight and rough treatment.

With the equipment tested, Drake moved on to the *Nautilus* itself. He stood inside and directed everyone to hurl buckets of water over the surface as

113

he sought out holes.

Benny had done his job well as no water got through, but that didn't appear to satisfy Drake as he worried over every inch of the interior, searching for dampness.

'Are we ever going to do this?' Benny asked finally, making Drake laugh.

'I knew I'd get you all enthused eventually,' Drake said. 'Now that you believe, I guess there's no point in delaying.'

With that, he signified that the *Nautilus* should be roped up so that it could be dragged on to the platform. As it turned out, this took longer than anyone expected.

There were no suitable protrusions on the outside to secure the ropes and so they resorted to wrapping rope around the car several times.

Then, although Randolph was already on the other side of the water with a team of horses, the first attempt to move the *Nautilus* merely tightened the rope while the car stayed where it was.

The sun had already reached its highest point by the time the car moved for the first time. It was only for a few scraping inches, but with this encouragement they placed logs in its path.

Once the *Nautilus* had moved on to the first log, it moved more readily. By the time they'd slipped a second, and then a third, log beneath it, the car moved along smoothly.

When it reached the platform, the *Nautilus* speeded up and so, fearing that it would keep sliding along until it fell off the end, they stopped moving logs round to the front.

This plan worked, although perhaps too well as the car ground to a halt on the wooden platform with the front still a yard from the end.

The *Nautilus* settled down with a groaning of timbers from its platform that sounded as if the car had found a permanent resting place. Drake called a halt to assess the situation.

It was now early afternoon, so everyone settled down to take a break and to eat, but Drake paced around in a determined way that Wyndham now recognized as being his way of planning what they should do next.

'We need to decide if we're going to try this today,' Wyndham said, joining him on the platform. 'After all, we don't want to be scuttling around underwater when Finnegan arrives.'

Drake glanced at the sun and nodded. 'I'll take care of Finnegan no matter when he arrives. The more important thing is that you believe this will work.'

'I do. You seem to be the one having second thoughts.'

'I'm not sure we'll be able to drag the *Nautilus* back on to the platform, so I'm thinking about a different way of doing this.'

'The water's not too deep here. Perhaps the *Nautilus* could sit on the bottom and we could get in and out through the roof instead of through the back.'

Drake slapped his back. 'I like your idea. I'll get Benny to see if he can do it.'

Drake hurried off the platform leaving Wyndham to tip back his hat and consider the water. He couldn't help but note that his heart was beating faster in anticipation of them soon trying out something that he had thought impossible.

Finnegan's imminent arrival somehow no longer felt so worrying, although he now hoped he wouldn't come today. That thought made him look beyond the group at the side of the water.

With a flinch he noticed movement, although when he located the source of the movement he noted that someone was heading upriver.

As this direction meant it couldn't be Finnegan, he didn't interrupt Drake and Benny's conversation and instead he clambered off the platform and moved on with his neck craned.

When he'd walked for a short distance, he identified the newcomer as being Seymour Banks.

Seymour had headed downriver a few days ago. With everything that had happened recently, that time now felt far longer.

'I expect you didn't have any luck,' Wyndham called.

Seymour didn't reply immediately as he considered the industry around the shore with bemusement. Then he stopped and waited for Wyndham to join him.

'I had an interesting time,' he said, 'but it looks as if you've had a more interesting one.'

'Marshal Drake has hatched a plan to reach the silver. It's a wild one, but he's got us all believing in him.'

Seymour snorted. 'That's certainly a skill that man has in abundance.'

'In the short time he's been here, he's changed the town. I had my doubts when Finnegan Kelly's hired guns shot up half the town, but even with Finnegan's arrival being. . . .'

Wyndham trailed off when Seymour glared over his shoulder at the group beside the water, his furrowed brow suggesting he wasn't listening to him.

'You need to get the townsfolk together and away from the marshal.'

'Why?'

'Because the only thing I know for sure is that the man you're all following isn't Marshal Drake.'

'How do you know that?'

'Because the marshal is dead.'

Wyndham looked at Seymour with an incredulous expression. When Seymour returned his gaze levelly, Wyndham swung round to look back at Drake. He nodded and then turned back to Seymour.

'He's been acting strangely and I've thought several times that he's not like any lawman I've ever met.'

Seymour nodded. 'I followed your instructions as I headed downriver and looked for areas where things wash up. I must have developed a knack for finding bodies as a few miles out of Black Town I found one. I got Sheriff Pollard's help and he identified it as being Marshal Drake's. He'd been shot.'

Wyndham pointed at the group. 'The man calling himself Marshal Drake has a star.'

'Presumably he took it off the real marshal, and here's the interesting thing. The marshal's mission was the one this man claimed to be carrying out: tracking down the survivors of the Kane Cresswell gang. Apparently, he was on the trail of the last member.'

'It sounds as if he found him.'

'It does, which just leaves the question of who is the man you've been calling Marshal Drake?'

CHAPTER 12

With Seymour at his side Wyndham headed back to the shore.

Drake was issuing orders and so Wyndham doubted he could get everyone away from him easily. Worse, Seymour's stern posture would be sure to alert him that something was wrong.

So Wyndham settled for catching Benny's eye with a long look. Then he swung to a halt in front of Drake while Seymour moved past him.

'We've got a problem,' he announced. 'Seymour headed downriver and he found another body.'

Drake frowned. 'That was always likely. I believe you had four friends who worked on the bridge and not all them have washed up yet.'

Wyndham jutted his jaw, as if he was considering this possibility, but Seymour had already heard enough. He advanced on Drake, giving Wyndham no choice but to act.

Seymour slapped a hand on Drake's shoulder and spun him round while Wyndham grabbed Drake's arm. Then they combined forces to bundle him to the ground.

Even with two men pressing down on him, Drake fought back strongly. He knocked Seymour aside and then Benny hurried in and tried to wrestle Wyndham away from him from behind.

'You can't attack a lawman,' Benny said as Drake strained to reach his gun.

'He's no lawman,' Wyndham said. 'He's fooled us all.'

Wyndham couldn't have been the only one in town who had doubts as the moment he'd made his claim, Quincy and Percy hurried in. They grabbed one leg apiece while Wyndham disarmed Drake and Benny pinned Drake's arms above his head.

Drake struggled, but with everyone holding him down, he could only wriggle ineffectually. Wyndham collected rope and they rolled him over to secure his hands behind his back.

They walked him to the platform and secured him to a corner post before stepping back to consider him.

'Who is he?' Benny asked after Drake had done nothing other than glare at them.

'I reckon he's a member of the Kane Cresswell gang,' Seymour said. 'In fact, he's probably the last member.'

Wyndham nodded. 'He told me plenty of stories about the relationship between Finnegan Kelly and Kane Cresswell, so if he told the truth about that, it would explain his actions.'

Wyndham raised an eyebrow, inviting a response, and this time Drake took the opportunity to reply.

'I told you more truths than lies, so believe this now. Release me and I'll deal with Finnegan.'

'You've asked us to believe a lot recently.' Wyndham gestured at the car. 'We built the *Nautilus* because of that belief.'

'Keep on believing that it'll work, and it will.'

Drake fixed Wyndham with a firm gaze, as if through sheer force of will he could make him release him.

'We might believe you, but only if you start being honest with us. Who are you?'

'I'm not a member of the Kane Cresswell gang.' He chuckled. 'I *am* Kane Cresswell.'

Wyndham sneered. 'Kane shot up my friend Ewan Douglas.'

'I didn't kill him, although he very nearly killed me.'

'No matter who fired the fatal bullet, it was your men who raided the train.'

'What I told you about the raid was the truth. Finnegan Kelly promised that the only people who would suffer was the railroad. The guards were paid to give up without a fight and you and your people were supposed to be elsewhere.'

Wyndham shrugged. 'Finnegan is as much to blame as you are, and so we'll be the ones who deal with him.'

'Don't. He double-crossed me and he can't get away with that.'

'It wasn't his fault that Ewan was on the train and it wasn't his fault the silver fell off the bridge.'

'I agree about your friend Ewan, but the strong-box falling off the bridge was down to him. I've had a long time to think about the moment when I tried to rescue the box, and I have a theory.' Kane glanced over his shoulder at the water and then shook his head. 'The silver isn't in the water over there.'

'It might not be, but it has to be somewhere in the river.'

'It doesn't, because I reckon it never fell into the water in the first place. Finnegan planned to trick me all along.'

'How do you know that?'

'The box fell off the back of the train and lurched to the side. I don't reckon it should have been that top-heavy. And I don't know what fifty thousand dollars' worth of silver sounds like, but I heard only thuds coming from inside the box.'

'You're saying Finnegan filled the box with rocks and he kept the money for himself?'

Kane nodded. 'That's my theory. As far as the rail-road is concerned, I tried to steal the money, but it was lost. They weren't to know that only a heap of rocks landed in the water.'

Wyndham pointed at the car. 'So why have we spent the last few days building something to look for the silver?'

'Because all I have is a theory and when Finnegan arrives, the *Nautilus* will help me prove what happened to the silver.'

Wyndham nodded. 'If Finnegan is worried that it might work, the silver must be in the river somewhere. If he's not worried about us finding something, that means the silver isn't down there.'

'That's why I need you to believe. If you're convinced this plan will work, Finnegan will believe it, too.'

'And when you've got to the truth?'

'I'll kill him, but shooting him up won't be enough. I want him to suffer like I did. I nearly drowned in the water. Then I tumbled over the falls and I nearly drowned again. I want him to know what that feels like.'

'You intend to throw him in the *Nautilus* and sink it.'

'I had hoped he might go in there voluntarily, but I'll settle for throwing him in.' Kane smiled. 'Let me go and nobody else need die in Silver Falls.'

Wyndham looked away while shaking his head. Then, with a long sigh, he told Percy and Quincy to watch Kane while he drew Seymour and Benny aside.

'You heard him,' he said. 'What do you think?'

'We shouldn't even consider this,' Seymour said. 'He's a protection man; his gang shot up your friend Ewan Douglas – and he probably killed the real Marshal Drake.'

Wyndham nodded and then turned to Benny.

'It could be even worse than that,' he said. 'We didn't work out how Norman Pierce died, and right now Kane's the most likely culprit.'

'Kane could have killed Norman because he'd worked out who he was,' Wyndham said. 'That's one crime we might be able to. . . . '

Wyndham trailed off as another worrying thought hit him. He swirled round to look at Kane, and his shocked expression must have explained everything as Benny carried out the same action.

They paced back to Kane, who registered that he'd seen them coming with a smile that died when he saw their thunderous expressions, giving Wyndham all the answers he needed.

'I guess you won't be letting me go,' he said.

Wyndham didn't trust himself to explain and so he settled for bunching a fist and slapping Kane's face backhanded, cracking his head to the side. The moment Kane straightened up, Wyndham thundered an even stronger round-armed punch to his other cheek that rocked his head the other way.

'The first punch was for Norman Pierce,' he said. 'The second punch was for Crosby Jensen. How many more times do I have to hit you before we reach the end of the list?'

Kane shrugged. 'I'm not sure my jaw or your fist will be able to take that.'

Kane's unconcerned attitude made Wyndham's blood race and the next he knew he'd wrapped both hands around Kane's throat and he was squeezing with all his might. Seymour and Benny moved in on him and grabbed one arm apiece, but he settled his stance and bunched his shoulders.

Kane met his gaze with a stoic glare that suggested Seymour and Benny were keeping him from closing his windpipe. He strained even harder, and a moment later a crack sounded. Then he and everyone else tumbled over.

He landed on the platform on his side. As he struggled his way clear from the entangled arms and legs, he worked out that the combined weight of the four men had made the corner post topple over.

Then he had other problems to deal with when Kane fought his way clear of the post and, with the ropes still constraining him, caught Wyndham's chin with a flailing elbow. Wyndham went down again and when he'd shook himself and sat up, it was to find that Seymour had been poleaxed while Kane and Benny were struggling.

Kane's hands were still loosely tied behind his back, but spurred on with manic energy, he thrust a shoulder down and barged into Benny. Then, with a mixture of shoving and kicking, he tipped Benny off the side of the platform and into the shallows.

Kane then looked around, but Wyndham had now shaken off the earlier blows and was reaching for his gun. Kane abandoned trying to run off the platform and instead he turned on his heel and ran along the side of car.

By the time he reached the end of the platform Wyndham had drawn and aimed his gun, but he stilled his fire when Kane slipped around the far end of the *Nautilus*. Percy hurried into the shallows to help Benny back to dry land, so Wyndham signified that Quincy should cover the other side of the car.

He moved purposefully along the platform. Kane had nowhere to go other than to leap into the water, but the water was swirling rapidly and Wyndham didn't think he'd risk making himself such an open target.

He moved on cautiously with his gun held before him and his gaze set on the end of the car. When Kane didn't make a move, he stopped two paces from the end.

'There's nowhere to run to, Kane,' he said.

He waited for an answer, and when one wasn't forthcoming he moved to the edge of the platform in case Kane was planning to attack him when he moved round to the front. Then he edged forward but, as more of the short space at the front of the platform became visible, he failed to see Kane.

The car didn't have a door at the front and so he assumed Kane was standing with his back to the front waiting for him. He stopped.

'If you try anything,' he said, 'I'll shoot you.'

Then he moved on, revealing the platform and then the front of the car, still with no sign of Kane.

He turned round to check that Quincy had stayed on land to cover the other side of the platform, and then to his irritation he saw that Quincy had turned his back on the *Nautilus.*

Worse, Benny and Percy weren't looking in his direction either.

Then he saw what had attracted their attention. Men were coming down the side of Silver Gorge.

'Finnegan Kelly,' Wyndham muttered to himself.

CHAPTER 13

'Finnegan won't get down here for several minutes,'
Wyndham called to Benny as he hurried towards dry
land. 'And we need to recapture Kane first.'

Benny turned to him and raised a hand to acknow-
ledge his order, but then he stopped and crouched
down. A moment later, in a blur of movement, Kane
sprinted off the platform and ran into Quincy, who
was still looking up the side of the gorge.

Both men went down, with Quincy hitting the
ground chest first and Kane bearing down on him.
Benny and Percy both trained guns on them, as did
Wyndham when he reached the end of the platform,
but Kane kept his wits about him.

He disarmed Quincy and then swung him up to
his feet. With one arm held across Quincy's chest he
held him from behind while he pressed the gun
against the side of his hostage.

'Lower those guns and save your bullets for

Finnegan,' he demanded.

'We don't need you to settle our differences with Finnegan,' Wyndham said.

'He's brought seven men with him and they're sure to be more fearsome gun-toters than any of you are. You'll never prevail. You need my help.'

'What you really mean is that you need our help to prevail. You want us to provide Finnegan's gunmen with target practice while you sit back and wait for things to get easier, like you did when Marvin came.'

Kane shrugged. 'That works for me, too.'

Benny looked at Wyndham and sneered, while Percy slowly shook his head. Wyndham was wondering how he could support them while not risking Quincy's life when he caught sight of the approaching men.

Finnegan's men had covered half the distance down to the bottom and so would reach them faster than he'd expected. They were spreading out in a way that suggested they had a plan in mind and so in an instant decision he raised his gun.

'And it works for me, too. We combine forces to get Finnegan.'

Benny opened his mouth to complain, but Wyndham raised a hand, silencing him while Kane helped the situation by shoving Quincy aside.

'Agreed,' he said.

'But only until this is over.'

'Of course.'

Kane tipped his hat and then swung round to look up the gorge. Wyndham tried to avoid everyone else's eye and moved towards Seymour, who was still lying where he'd fallen after his tussle with Kane.

Wyndham shook his shoulders and then slapped his cheeks until he stirred, although Seymour still looked up at him with glazed eyes.

'We have to stop Kane,' he murmured, his voice sounding groggy.

'We don't,' Wyndham said. 'We're all fighting on the same side now.'

Seymour winced. 'How long have I been lying here?'

Wyndham smiled and then helped Seymour to his feet, by which time the approaching danger had taken Benny's and Percy's minds off their disagreement with him. They, along with Quincy, joined him on the platform to consider the situation.

The men weren't close enough yet for Wyndham to work out which one was Finnegan and they were slowing as they used the available cover of the trees.

Several men were to the left of the main trail, ensuring that if they retreated downriver these men could cut them off easily, leaving them with no choice but to stay put and defend their position.

He considered the substantial bulk of the *Nautilus* at their backs and without further comment they clambered up on to the platform attached to the back of the car. Billy had reinforced the car with wood around the platform, giving them cover, while he'd made the door half its normal height and secured at the base to help make the interior watertight.

From this elevated position Wyndham felt more confident because when the gunmen approached they would have to move over open ground while he and his compadres could look down at them. Kane glanced their way, but he didn't join them and hunkered down behind the pile of debris they'd created while building the *Nautilus*.

Their tactic made the men stop and glance to the centre of the line they'd formed, letting Wyndham identify Finnegan. He leaned over the back of the car.

'Finnegan's the third man from the right,' he called to Kane, who raised himself to pick out this man before ducking down.

The others shot aggrieved glances at Wyndham, but he ignored them and settled down to let Finnegan make the first move.

As it turned out, fifteen minutes passed quietly as the gunmen took it in turns to move cautiously down the lower part of the slope.

They took up final positions behind the last piece of available cover – a fallen tree – before the flat stretch of land that led to the water. Finnegan raised himself several times to consider the scene, and he paid especial consideration to the car.

'After I closed the station, you people appear to have lost your minds,' he called, breaking the tense silence. 'Moving a worm-eaten old car down here is utter madness.'

'It isn't,' Wyndham called. 'We did that because we've got our senses back.'

Bearing in mind his earlier conversation with Kane, he didn't explain their actions. He hoped that when he revealed their reason, he would be able to see Finnegan's reaction and so work out the truth about the silver.

'You may think you're safe hiding behind the *marshal,* but you're not.'

Wyndham noted Finnegan's emphasis and that made him smile as a second small advantage revealed itself. The sight of the car down here had clearly wrong-footed Finnegan, and he planned to reveal the marshal's true identity at a crucial moment in the hope that it'd buy him an advantage.

'He'll come for us now,' Wyndham whispered to the others.

Everyone returned sombre nods, their eyes now less accusing than they had been earlier, and their postures became alert when a few moments later Wyndham's prediction came true.

Reacting to a signal from Finnegan, presumably, the two men who were holed up furthest to the left ran down to the water, aiming for a position fifty yards downriver of the platform.

At the same moment the two men furthest to the right carried out the same manoeuvre, this time aiming for a position between the platform and the falls. They ran briskly with their heads down, taking a direct route.

Percy and Quincy followed the men on their side with their guns and Benny and Seymour followed the men on their side. In the middle Wyndham joined Kane in aiming at Finnegan and his two gunmen, who had stayed put.

Everyone held their fire until the men had halved the distance to the water. Then, just as Wyndham was preparing to give the order to fire, Finnegan and the two men to either side launched a ferocious burst of gunfire.

From such a distance Wyndham had expected them to try to keep Kane subdued, but instead they fired at the car, and the first volley pinged into the wood a foot below the edge on which they were leaning.

Wyndham hoped that they'd just got lucky and he aimed at the nearest running man, but the gunmen had just been getting them in their sights and the second volley tore into the car.

Quincy cried out, his gun falling from his grasp as he fell forward to lie over the back of the car with his arms dangling. The others dropped down and Percy tugged on Quincy's jacket, making him slide back into the car.

The sight of the hole in his forehead made them all turn away.

'If the gunmen could hit him from the other side of the clearing,' Percy said, 'what chance do we have?'

'None, if we don't fight back,' Wyndham said.

With that, he raised himself, but he avoided the back of the car and looked to the side. He couldn't see the gunmen who had been running for the water and so he presumed that they'd holed up behind one of the numerous boulders that littered the shore.

Seymour took the other side and he reported that the situation was the same, and so Benny risked bobbing up to look over the back.

'Same again,' he reported unhappily. 'Except it's worse. Finnegan's group has moved and I can't see where they've gone.'

'What about Kane?'

Seymour shrugged and so Wyndham moved to the back. Kane was no longer hiding behind the pile of debris, but, with gunmen now on both sides, that position would no longer have been safe.

He trained his gun from side to side, looking for movement as he tried to put Quincy's demise from his mind and make full use of their elevated position. His confidence encouraged the others to rise up and this time Benny took the right and Percy the left while Seymour stood at his side.

For long moments he saw no movement and when he did catch a hint that something was amiss, it came from a pile of wood twenty yards away. The light on the ground to the side was changing, presumably from someone moving behind the wood.

He caught Seymour's attention and he craned his neck and then smiled.

'Now that's where Kane's gone,' he said. 'And he appears to be waving.'

'He must be trying to tell us something. But what?'

Seymour frowned, but they got their answer soon enough when Kane leapt to his feet. He fired a shot to either side and then, with his head down, they saw him sprint for the platform.

Despite their earlier disagreements, Benny and Percy both covered him by laying down gunfire to either side, while Seymour and Wyndham fired over the back. They had no visible targets to aim at, but they achieved the desired result when Kane reached the platform without retaliation.

Even so, Kane wasted no time in leaping on to the platform. Seymour and Wyndham held out a hand and helped him clamber up on to the back of the car, and then he joined them in looking over the back.

'Nobody could survive out there with gunmen on every side,' he said. 'So I thought I'd join you up here.'

'We could see you signalling,' Wyndham said. 'I assume that was to tell us to put aside our differences and cover you.'

'The signals weren't meant for you. I was getting Randolph's attention on the other side of the water.'

'He's too far away to help us, and by the time he gets round here we'll probably all be dead.'

'You're right about that, so I changed the plan.'

Kane raised an eyebrow, and a few moments later a creaking sounded nearby, suggesting what the new plan was.

'What did you tell him to do?' Wyndham still asked, hoping he'd misunderstood, but Kane smiled.

'I reckon,' he said, 'it's time for the maiden voyage of the *Nautilus*.'

CHAPTER 14

'You can't be serious,' Wyndham spluttered as the others muttered similar comments.

'We're facing a whole heap of gunslingers and even I might not prevail against them,' Kane said. He pointed at Quincy's body. 'We need to get away or we'll all end up like him.'

'We can't get away on this. You never meant the *Nautilus* to actually go into the water. It was just a way to get Finnegan to reveal the truth.'

'I might not have intended the *Nautilus* to move off this platform, but you all did. I guess in the next few minutes we'll find out just how good a job you did.'

Wyndham stared at Kane, still hoping that he was again using his ability to lie convincingly, but Kane returned his gaze while a swishing noise outside provided the impression that Randolph was tightening the ropes.

'Get shot up or get drowned.' Wyndham sighed. 'That's not much of a choice.'

'We don't have to drown. After all, it's easier to hold your breath when you're not full of holes.'

When Kane smiled, Wyndham waved a dismissive hand at him and looked at the others for their opinions, but they just returned sorry shakes of the head. Then, with resigned airs, they returned to their former positions to keep watch in all directions.

Wyndham returned to looking out the back while Kane busied himself with swinging up the half-door, this being the only entrance to what Wyndham now viewed as a huge coffin.

Creaks and swishes continued to sound, but the car didn't move, giving Wyndham hope that Kane's reckless plan might not even get started. But their escape attempt must have looked suitably believable as the men to either side appeared briefly from behind their covering boulders to survey their scene.

Before anyone could fire at them they returned behind cover, but they must have signalled to Finnegan as he emerged from hiding behind a fallen tree. With his men on either side they fired at the car while sprinting for the debris where Kane had holed up earlier.

With the men running, their shots weren't as well aimed as before and Wyndham wasn't sure where they landed, so he aimed at Finnegan. Seymour and Kane both stayed up to join him in aiming at the two men and they managed one shot apiece before the gunmen either side laid down covering fire.

The men in the car all fired at once and they dispatched one of the running men with a shot that sliced into his stomach and made him keel over. Heartened by their success, they loosed off another volley while Finnegan and the other man gave up on firing at them and concentrated on reaching cover.

The men to either side started up a sustained barrage of lead, but with Finnegan getting closer with every step, Wyndham grew in confidence and he steadied his aim, determined to make his next shot count. Then the car lurched.

The sudden motion made everyone in the car jerk while Percy moved into the open space on his side. He had yet to get his balance when a deadly shot thundered into his chest and he went spinning round before falling over.

As the car shuddered to a halt, Benny checked on him and shook his head. By the time they returned to considering the scene outside, Finnegan had gone to ground.

Seymour took over Percy's position, leaving Kane and Wyndham looking at the pile of debris. With everyone then staying down, Wyndham looked out of the back at the platform.

He could see no sign of the car having moved, but the ropes below were taut and the corner of the platform where they'd broken the post was at an angle to the land.

When long moments had passed in silence, he looked at Kane.

'We've not moved again for a while,' he said. 'I don't reckon we're going anywhere.'

'It was always likely, but Finnegan's not to know that.' Kane smiled and then raised his voice. 'Hey, Finnegan, you want to join us?'

'That car's too heavy,' Finnegan called while keeping his head down. 'It'll never move.'

'It already has. We're slowly moving away already.'

'Then you'll just sink.'

'I hope so. It's what the *Nautilus* is designed to do.' Kane waited for a response, but Finnegan stayed silent. 'We intend to use it to look for the silver.'

This final taunt made Finnegan raise himself for a moment before ducking down.

'I don't know what you're really aiming to do with that car, but that's not the plan.'

Kane smirked and Wyndham nodded approvingly. He leaned towards Kane.

'You've rattled him,' he said.

Kane nodded and, adding further proof to his claim, the *Nautilus* lurched again. This time a crack sounded across the platform and Wyndham noted that both sides of the platform were now leaning away from land.

Even as he watched they leaned further away,

giving him the impression that Randolph was succeeding in pulling the car towards the other side of the water, but he was doing so only by moving the platform, too.

'It sure is,' Kane shouted. 'We located the strongbox. It came to rest forty yards into the water where nobody could get to it, but we have a plan to retrieve the contents.'

'I wish you luck, and when you return I'll be waiting here to claim the silver off you.'

'You'll fail.' Kane coughed. 'Although, of course, if the strongbox is only full of rocks, we'll leave it out there.'

Wyndham tensed and sure enough that taunt was clearly too close to the truth as Finnegan appeared briefly to gesture at the gunmen at either side. A moment later lead hammered into either side of the car, forcing both Benny and Seymour to sway away.

Wyndham and Kane kept their guns trained on the debris, waiting for Finnegan to show, but he kept his head down and when Benny next risked looking out, he flinched back quickly with a shocked expression on his face.

'They've reached the platform,' he said.

Wyndham peered out of the back and looked down, seeing the men hunkered down beside the platform. The men swung their guns towards him and so he moved back quickly.

'They're ready to take us,' Wyndham said. 'I

reckon the only thing keeping them back is they don't know what will happen to the *Nautilus*.'

The platform lurched again, accompanied by another crack. This time Wyndham felt sure the land was further away than before and it may have been his nervous state, but he also felt as if the *Nautilus* was leaning down towards the water.

'None of us know that,' Kane said, 'but I reckon it's time to find out.'

He gestured at the open half-door, making them all consider it. Nobody moved, giving the impression that they were all waiting for someone else to be the first to put their fate in the hands of their creation.

Gunfire rattled outside and at least two shots sliced by before ricocheting off the roof and then winging their way outside. Wyndham reckoned the shooting was the prelude to an attack and so he made for the door.

Kane snorted a supportive laugh while Benny and Seymour murmured in surprise. Once Wyndham had slipped his legs inside, he hunched over so he could slip through the door with a quick movement, and then looked up at them.

'It's the only way,' he said. 'Inside, we can sit this out and hope for the best.'

'We don't know if it's fully waterproof,' Benny said.

'The only thing on my mind is whether it's bullet-proof.'

Wyndham gave Benny and Seymour a long look. Then, figuring he'd said enough and what they did now was their decision, he ducked down and slipped into the *Nautilus*.

Aside from the light coming through the door, the only other light came through the window Benny had installed at the front, but it was enough for Wyndham to make his way along. He stood up and turned round, but nobody had followed him through the door.

The *Nautilus* jerked and, when he looked to the front, he could see the river through the window. With a sudden change of perspective he felt as if he were leaning forward and the car was in imminent danger of toppling over into the water.

Consternation erupted behind him with raised voices and two quick gunshots. Then Benny came scrambling through the door with Seymour close behind him.

Seymour shuffled forward until he could stand up, but Benny stayed by the door. Another gunshot sounded and then Kane dived through the doorway.

He rolled on to his front and the moment he drew his legs up, Benny grabbed the top of the door, aiming to bring it down and seal them inside. He had yet to move it when one of the gunmen leapt inside and slammed down on Kane's chest.

Kane tried to wrestle his assailant away, but

143

another man followed him through the door and joined the other man in pinning him down while another man slipped through and grabbed Benny.

Seymour hurried on to join Wyndham and they both aimed at the doorway, but the *Nautilus* was bucking around so much they struggled to keep their balance and Wyndham feared that if he fired he could hit Benny or Kane.

Wyndham moved over to put a hand to one wall to steady himself and Seymour followed his lead in taking the other side. That made Wyndham feel steadier, but unfortunately the struts that Benny had installed and which now strengthened the walls were between him and the fighting men.

He stilled his fire, as did the next two men to slip through the door. Finnegan came in last and he looked down the length of the *Nautilus* at Wyndham.

'I received an offer to join you,' Finnegan said. 'So I thought I'd see your strange vessel for myself.'

'I'm surprised,' Wyndham said. 'I thought you said that it was too heavy and it wouldn't move.'

'It won't. The ropes are straining and everything out there is creaking and swinging around, but this car is moored solidly on the platform and it's not going anywhere.'

Wyndham glanced over his shoulder at the window. The view of the river hadn't changed, adding credence to Finnegan's claim.

'Then why have you come in here?'

'To take your marshal away.' Finnegan chuckled. 'Let me have him and you can go wherever you like in your car.'

Wyndham moved so he could see Kane, who was still struggling, but he was being effectively pinned down while another gunman held a gun on him.

Worse, Benny was then thrown up against the wall and a gun was slapped against his side.

'He knows the truth about what happened here three months ago,' Wyndham said. 'We can't let you have him.'

'That man knows nothing about the truth.'

'He knows plenty. It was his idea to build this vessel and I reckon it'll work.'

Finnegan snorted. 'How can you say that when you don't even know the most basic fact about him?'

'I know that's he's no marshal. He's Kane Cresswell, a man you double-crossed.' Wyndham shrugged. 'And this vessel will find out the truth about the missing silver.'

Finnegan's eyes flared with what Wyndham took to be genuine surprise, but before Wyndham could enjoy his success in shocking him, he suffered the strange feeling of tipping over even though he was standing upright. Then he registered that Finnegan was looking past him at the window.

Wyndham turned and with a gulp he saw that despite Finnegan's earlier pronouncement, the *Nautilus* was now moving smoothly and the water was only feet away from the window.

Then the *Nautilus* slid down into the river with a groan.

CHAPTER 15

The light level in the *Nautilus* plummeted in a moment.

Wyndham lost his balance and went to his knees, only the hand he held to the side of the car letting him control his descent.

The others didn't fare so well.

Scrambling and curses sounded as everyone tumbled over and then went scooting along the bottom of the car. Wyndham looked for Benny amongst them, but he could make out only the dark outlines of people.

He looked for Seymour and he had better luck when he found him on the other side of the *Nautilus*. Seymour had adopted the same posture of kneeling down while looking around.

When Seymour saw that Wyndham was looking at him, he pointed at three men who were backing away into the space between them.

These men were entangled and they appeared to be struggling to stay upright. When they moved closer, Wyndham's eyes had become more accustomed to the poor light, letting him see that Kane was trying to fight off two of Finnegan's men.

He and Seymour exchanged nods. Then, in a co-ordinated move, they got up and advanced on the gunmen.

Kane must have seen them coming as he redoubled his efforts and tore himself free, giving Wyndham enough room to grab the nearest man's arm and hurl him aside.

Seymour batted his opponent over on to his back with a wild lunge of an arm. Then, with both opponents floundering, they looked for others to take on.

Unfortunately, it was becoming darker by the moment. Wyndham could no longer see the back of the *Nautilus* and he even struggled to distinguish people if they weren't moving, so he couldn't identify either Finnegan or Benny.

The others were clearly having the same problem as nobody was moving with any purpose, and so when Kane slapped his arm and pointed at the window, he didn't complain. He got Seymour's attention and then the three men made their way to the front of the car.

Through the window Wyndham could see only swirling brown murk, providing the impression that the *Nautilus* was working as intended by ploughing through the water. Almost as if it then came to confirm this observation, cold water slapped against his ankles.

Muttered complaints broke out around the *Nautilus* as the water rose up to his knees quickly. Wyndham couldn't see any leaks along the walls, so he assumed the water was coming in through the door at the back.

He figured if the *Nautilus* had no other leaks, the water should rise no higher than his waist and so he turned to Kane.

'I guess you're to be congratulated,' he said.

'I only had the idea,' Kane said. 'You folks built this.'

Their brief conversation appeared to help the other men get a sense of direction as everyone turned to the front. The men spread out around the car and Finnegan identified himself by speaking up from the back.

'Your contraption hasn't worked,' he muttered. 'It just broke through the platform and sank, taking us with it.'

Finnegan kicked at the water, as if he could drive it away by the force of his anger, but the water was still rising and, as it crept up to Wyndham's thighs, Finnegan stopped moving.

'We can survive down here,' Kane said. 'Provided we stay calm and don't do anything to wreck the *Nautilus*.'

'So what you're saying is gunfire could hole your infernal machine and let water in?'

'That would be the best result. The worst is lead zinging around in here until it finds a body to bury itself in.'

Finnegan grunted, affirming this was the most likely result, and then slapped the shoulders of the two men closest to him. He whispered quick instructions and then they waded through the water towards the front of the *Nautilus*.

Every few steps the men gathered the others about them until a wall of men were moving down the car as they clearly planned to overcome them with superior numbers. They were half way to the front of the car when their progress helped Wyndham to identify which form was Benny's.

He had been lying hunched over by the side and when one man slapped his shoulder, Benny came up quickly and then tussled with his assailant. Wyndham couldn't see who was getting the upper hand, but then a crunch sounded followed by a long scraping sound.

Wyndham assumed the *Nautilus* had reached the bottom of the river, but they were still being dragged along.

With the *Nautilus* lurching badly, Wyndham had to fight to stay upright while Benny used the movements to hurl his opponent aside. Then he made for the front.

The moment he was clear of the other men Seymour started shooting. One man cried out as his shot found a target and this initiated a returning volley of gunshots.

Perhaps because they'd wrongly identified the first shooter as being Kane, most of the lead hammered into Seymour, who went toppling over on to his back in the water.

Not all the shots found their targets and, as Kane had feared, lead went whistling off the walls, sending up sparks as the slugs hit the metal struts Benny had added.

Another man cried out as a stray bullet found a target and, when Wyndham felt his hat kick as a bullet came close, he dropped down into the water.

Kneeling down, the water came up to his armpits and he had to raise his arms to keep his gun dry.

From the corner of his eye he saw Benny make the same defensive move, but Kane stayed standing. He blasted off round after round at the massed ranks of the gunmen and, as Wyndham heard few ricochets, most of his shots found a target.

Wyndham reckoned he saw three men go down before someone got Kane in their sights. A low shot to the stomach made Kane fold over while a second shot winged his arm and made him stagger away to slam into the wall beside the window.

'You got him,' Finnegan shouted. 'Now wipe out the rest.'

Water splashed into Wyndham's eyes ensuring that in the gloom he couldn't work out where Finnegan had delivered his order. Worse, he was in an awkward position with most of his body underwater, so he doubted he could hit a target even if he could find one.

Wyndham dropped down to submerge his head beneath the water. He stayed down until his lungs demanded air and then cautiously came up, and it was to get a clear view of Finnegan and Kane.

They were standing before the window, the small amount of light filtering in showing their forms in harsh relief. Kane had grabbed Finnegan's gun arm and he was trying to keep Finnegan from turning his gun on him, but blood glistened on Kane's jacket and Wyndham doubted he'd keep him at bay for long.

Wyndham couldn't see anyone else. So, surprising himself with the sudden decision, he got up and waded through the water to help Kane take on Finnegan.

The water had now reached past his waist and he could hear a gushing sound behind him, suggesting that some of the gunshots had created leaks.

His progress was slow and by the time he reached the window Kane was bent over as he struggled to ward off Finnegan.

Wyndham had become used to seeing only murk through the window and so he couldn't help but

152

shout out in surprise when he saw something outside.

A moment later the object came into focus.

'It's the strongbox,' he shouted.

Finnegan looked past Kane at the angular object emerging from out of the murky waters, while Kane summoned the strength to raise his head.

'We've found it,' Kane said. 'But what's inside?'

Finnegan snarled in anger and then dragged his gun arm clear of Kane's grip. With Finnegan moving away from Kane, Wyndham used the opportunity to lower his gun and shoot.

His accurate shot sliced into Finnegan's side, but that didn't stop Finnegan firing a single shot at the box that cracked through the centre of the window. The glass shattered and a moment later a wall of water slapped into Wyndham's side.

Wyndham went splashing down to the base of the car without gathering even a single breath and so he fought for balance so he could raise his head. He managed to get his head above water and draw in a breath and the better light at the front let him orient himself.

Kane and Finnegan had moved to the side of the window where both the badly wounded men had their hands around each other's throats, while beside them water poured into the car.

The water was already up to the window and after the initial deluge the rate of flow was less powerful.

Wyndham couldn't see anyone else and so he set his head down low and waded his way forward.

He managed five short steps, but by the sixth the water was up to his neck and before he could force himself forward again another wave of water washed over his head.

He craned his neck to try to stand clear, but he failed and so he reverted to using swimming strokes.

He pumped his arms until his feet raised themselves from the base and then he drove forward with both legs and arms. The current was still against him and he didn't feel as if he was making progress, but he figured that this at least meant he was trying to move in the right direction.

His lungs tightened as they demanded air and panic battered at his thoughts, making his lunges become more desperate. Then a hand clamped around something that yielded and a moment later a face appeared before him.

He could just make out wide-open eyes and that was enough for him to identify Benny. He locked hands with him and tugged, but Benny tugged in the opposite direction.

They strained, but with both men suspended in the water they achieved nothing other than to turn around each other. Wyndham was sure he was going in the right direction and so he fought to swim against the water surging in through the window.

Benny appeared to accept this when he stopped

fighting him. Their hands separated, but by now the need for air consumed all of Wyndham's thoughts.

Worse, he no longer had the strength to fight a current that appeared to be getting stronger by the moment.

Wyndham surrendered himself to the prevailing water flow and let it take him where it would, hoping that it would take him to the back of the *Nautilus* where he could get out through the door. But he moved on for what felt like far further than the length of the car without hitting the back.

Weirdly, the brown water that surrounded him started getting lighter below him.

He peered at the light while fighting to keep his lips closed. Then, in a disorientating moment, he registered that he was lying on his back and the light was above him.

With what felt like his last reserve of strength he thrust downwards and, in a surge, he emerged from the water, gasping and clawing in air.

Even as he enjoyed the cool air, he boggled at the unexpected sight of the low sun shining over the surface of the water.

Without him realizing it, he had swum out through the window and reached the surface. He trod water, struggling to work out how close to land he was.

A few moments later Benny broke the surface. Benny gasped and peered around while sporting the same shocked look that Wyndham assumed he was presenting.

Wyndham swam over to him and while treading water they faced each other.

'You reckon we're the only ones who got out?' Benny shouted over the roaring water.

'The last I saw of Kane and Finnegan, they were still trying to kill each other.' Wyndham swam round until he faced the falls and then looked down to where he thought the *Nautilus* would be. 'But it's yet to be proved whether we survived.'

Benny grunted that he agreed before they concentrated on trying to reach the side. Once Wyndham had worked out where in the water they were he calmed and to his instructions they conserved their energy and didn't fight the current.

When they reached the spot where Wyndham had cast the rope across the river, they started swimming. Just as the rope had done, with little effort on their parts, they fetched up in a tangle of trees.

Fifteen minutes later they clambered on to dry land, after which they made their cautious way back upriver.

When they reached the falls, they stood beside the remnants of the platform and watched the water, but they didn't see any sign of anyone else having come out.

The scene was so peaceful that a newcomer wouldn't be able to tell the gunfight had ever happened.

The car was beneath the water and only the unused parts left strewn about the area provided any hints of their efforts over the last few days. Randolph was still on the other side of the river and with gestures and shrugs he confirmed that he'd seen nobody else come out of the water.

Then he held up the end of the rope, signifying that it had snapped.

'I guess that means the *Nautilus* won't be completing its maiden voyage,' Benny said.

'And I reckon,' Wyndham said, 'that means Captain Nemo went down with his ship, again.'

CHAPTER 16

The delegation from the railroad was different from the last one.

Wyndham had seen some of the people before and he knew them to be Finnegan's superiors. Better still, they were all smiling.

The last few weeks had been peaceful.

After the gunfight the survivors had frequently gone down to the falls, but nobody else had come out of the water. After two days, they were sure that nobody else had survived and so they had contacted the railroad and relayed everything they knew about the situation.

Wyndham had hoped for a swift response. Accordingly, when the next train had been due Wyndham, Benny and Randolph had gathered at the station.

The train had trundled by, as had the next three, but nearly three weeks after Finnegan's demise, the train had stopped here again.

'We've completed our investigation,' one man said. 'Finnegan Kelly had kept the silver for himself. We're here to show our gratitude to whoever uncovered his crimes.'

When the man patted his pocket confirming the gratitude would have a financial element, Benny uttered a whoop of delight. Then he beckoned the delegation to join him in the Station Saloon.

The group followed and Wyndham had no doubt that Benny would provide them with so much liquor, by the time they were ready to leave he would have secured other advantages beyond the reward.

Even so, Wyndham was unsure if he'd be able to talk them into opening the station, but then he noticed that two people who had alighted from the train hadn't followed Benny.

He headed over to them and beckoned them to join him in going to the saloon, but they shook their heads.

'We're not with that group,' one man said. 'But we are looking for someone.'

These were the first people to come here looking for the silver since Kane Cresswell had arrived and their presence made him frown. He hadn't considered until now just how much he'd enjoyed taking people down to the falls.

'I'd guess that person is me. I used to charge a dollar a day to show visitors where the silver fell, but things have changed recently.' He pointed at the men who were heading into the saloon. 'Those railroad folk came here to confirm the silver has been found.'

'We know that, but we're not interested in the silver. We wanted someone to show us where Captain Nemo died.'

'Captain Nemo?' Wyndham spluttered.

'Yes. On the maiden voyage of the *Nautilus*.'

'The *Nautilus*?'

'Yes. Perhaps you know of someone who knows where it happened.'

Wyndham blinked rapidly and then shook off his surprise.

'I'm sorry for my confusion, but I was there on the day it happened and I can tell you, as an avid reader of Jules Verne, I was especially excited to bear witness to the momentous event.'

Both men grinned and as the train lurched to a start they joined Wyndham in heading off the platform.

'Can we actually see the *Nautilus*?'

'Perhaps not. It did go under the water, after all, but then again, like in the book Captain Nemo hasn't been seen since.'

'So maybe he could still be living down there somewhere?'

Wyndham leaned forward to wink. 'Maybe.'